Also by the Author

First Love

The Erin O'Reilly Mysteries
Book Ten

Steven Henry

Clickworks Press • Baltimore, MD

First publication: Clickworks Press, 2020
Release: CWP-EOR10-INT-P.IS-1.2

Sign up for updates, deals, and exclusive sneak peeks at clickworkspress.com/join.

Ebook ISBN: 978-1-943383-70-2
Paperback ISBN: 978-1-943383-71-9
Hardcover ISBN: 978-1-943383-72-6

For my first love, Jenny; we gave it our best shot.

First Love

Pour 2/3 oz. of champagne, 1/3 oz. of gin, 1 tsp of sugar, and 2 dashes of Heering Cherry Liqueur into a cocktail shaker half-filled with ice cubes. Shake well. Strain into a cocktail glass and serve.

Chapter 1

"Would you care for a glass of champagne, darling?"

"You've got champagne in there?"

Erin O'Reilly raised an eyebrow at the picnic basket. It looked like the full romantic deal. The wicker basket sat on a checkered cloth under a couple of parasols. There were even a pair of comfy-looking pillows to sit on and a single red rose.

"I believe it's part of the package, aye," Morton Carlyle said. "The fine folks who provide the service offered a carriage ride into the bargain, but I thought you'd consider that a bit much."

"I don't know," she said. "No one's ever bought me a carriage ride before."

They were in Central Park, on Cherry Hill, overlooking Bow Bridge. It was the sort of spot that made Erin think of fairy tales and rom-com movies. This wasn't a side of Manhattan she was accustomed to seeing. But she had to admit, as Carlyle opened the picnic basket and started laying out food, it had been a good idea.

Her only real concern was that someone might recognize them. After all, New York had eight million people in it, so of course they'd be bound to run into someone familiar. The probability might be low, but the stakes were high. Erin was a cop, a Major Crimes detective, and Carlyle was a mid-level organized crime associate. If they got spotted by the wrong person, Erin's career could be over. If they got spotted by an even worse person, both of them could get killed.

That was why Erin had brought two guns and her partner along on their romantic picnic lunch. Her primary sidearm, a Glock nine-millimeter, was holstered on her hip. Her backup piece, a snub-nosed .38 revolver, nestled in an ankle clip under her slacks. And her partner was flopped on his belly on the grass, tongue hanging out, grinning at her.

"What're you looking at?" she asked Rolf. The K-9 cocked his head in the endlessly endearing German Shepherd style.

"He's looking well," Carlyle said.

"Yeah. His hair's growing back."

"And the burns?"

"It's been a month. He's fine." Rolf and Erin were both carrying some scars from their last big case, which had culminated in a struggle in a burning movie theater. They'd gotten out of it okay, but not without a few mementos.

"And yourself, darling? How are you?"

"Hungry." She settled herself on one of the cushions. "What've we got here?"

"We've all manner of fine meats and cheeses, and what looks to be olives, nuts, and a grand loaf of fresh bread. Not to mention fruit and chocolate. What more could a lass be wanting?"

"Got any whiskey?"

He laughed. "Only the champagne, sad to say. But if you're wanting a wee nip, we could always slip back to the Corner after."

"I have to get back to work," she said. "This is just a long lunch, remember."

"This city's criminals have no sense of romance," he sighed. "Present company excepted, naturally."

Erin helped herself to some of the food, assembling a sandwich. Rolf watched with interest. He was too proud to beg, but there was always the possibility the humans might not want all the cold cuts.

"I'm sorry I've been so busy," she said. "It's all this petty bureaucratic bullshit. We haven't had a real takedown in a while."

"Are you bored, darling?"

"Yeah, a little. You know me. I live for the action." She took a bite. "You've got to try this pastrami. It's fantastic."

Carlyle sampled it. "Ah, that's grand. Are you well mended, yourself?"

She held up a hand and wiggled her fingers. "Everything's where it's supposed to be."

"You've hit it off well with my lad Ian. He tells me you and he are still running together most mornings."

"You're not jealous, are you?" she teased.

"Ought I to be?"

"You tell me. He's a handsome former Marine with a body a lot of guys would kill for. He's got that whole strong, silent thing going. He's polite. And the tattoos give him that exotic appeal."

Carlyle laughed. "A fine effort, lass, but I know both of you better than that."

"Ian's a good guy," she said, and meant it. Ian was Carlyle's driver and occasional bodyguard, a combat veteran who'd been a sniper in Iraq and Afghanistan. Carlyle had once called him the most dangerous man in New York, but Erin had come to feel safe around him.

A lot of that could be traced to the shared experience of trauma. One thing Erin hadn't told Carlyle was that she'd been wrestling with some bad memories lately. She'd started seeing the Precinct 8 police psychologist, Doc Evans, when the nightmares had gotten to be too much to handle. She knew Ian dealt with some of the same things from his war experiences, and knowing that had built a bridge of respect and trust between them. He'd protected her a couple of times in the past, and she trusted him as much as she did any fellow officer at her precinct.

The thought crossed her mind that she hadn't trusted Carlyle himself with the knowledge of her post-traumatic stress. But she pushed that to the back of her mind. There were all sorts of things he wasn't telling her, about his criminal associates and activities, because disclosure would do more harm than good to their relationship. Erin and Carlyle lived in a world where knowledge was both powerful and dangerous, and therefore needed to be guarded. They didn't ascribe to twenty-first century pop-psychology ideas of full openness between romantic partners. Otherwise, they wouldn't have gotten as far as they had.

"I'm glad you like him," Carlyle said. "He's rather fond of you, I'm thinking."

"How can you tell?"

"If he wasn't, he'd hardly keep going for morning runs with you. He'd have varied his route and you'd be unable to find him. If the lad wants to go unnoticed, I doubt even your partner would be able to track him."

"So you're not even a little jealous?" she prodded with a smile.

"Some lads might think this line of questioning indicated a bit of insecurity," he shot back. "Nay, darling. I love you. When a lad truly loves a lass, jealousy doesn't even enter his mind. Jealousy is for people who are afraid of losing someone. I know you're mine."

"I'm yours, huh? We'll see about that."

"The picnic lad offered me a surprise photographer as well," he commented. "But I thought that mightn't be the best idea. I told him if a lad sprang out of the bushes with something in his hands, you'd likely shoot him dead on the spot. He laughed."

"He probably thought you were joking," she said. "That's what I love about you."

"My sense of humor?"

"You understand me. They say only cops understand other cops, but we found a loophole."

"I'm good at loopholes," he said, smiling. "Believe me, darling, if there's any way out of a tangle, I'll thread my way through it."

"What if there isn't?" she asked. "What if we come to a dead end?"

"A lad's got to die sometime. In that case, the best we can hope is to make it mean something, and perhaps leave something worth remembering behind us. We're none of us getting out of this world alive."

"But we're alive here and now," she said. "How about cracking open that champagne and giving this girl a drink?"

*   *   *

Erin walked back into the Eightball, the Precinct 8 station, feeling pretty good. Her life was more or less back on track. The nightmares weren't as frequent as they had been. She was doing good work. While what she'd told Carlyle was true, they'd still closed some cases, busted some perps. However, as Vic Neshenko had pointed out, the bad guys hadn't quite fit the strict definition of "Major Crimes."

"Look who's back," Vic said. The big Russian was finishing his own lunch, chow mein takeout, washed down with a gigantic cup of Mountain Dew.

"Miss me?" she asked, sitting down at her desk.

"Yeah, but after I put in some time on the firing range, next time I won't."

"Promises," she said with a smile. "Anything happen while I was out?"

"We got a flag from Interpol," Vic said.

"Really? What about?"

"Remember that Finneran chick?"

The bottom dropped out of Erin's stomach. She wasn't likely to forget Siobhan Finneran. Siobhan's father had been a friend and comrade of Carlyle's, back when he'd been in the IRA in the early '90s. When Mr. Finneran had been killed, Carlyle had become her de facto father. Siobhan and Erin had disliked one another at first sight, and further association had only made things worse. Siobhan saw Erin as a rival for Carlyle's attention. She was a natural killer who'd learned from the best IRA assassins. The last time they'd met, Erin had been with an ESU team that had tried to arrest the other woman, only for Siobhan to vanish from New York for the second time.

"Yeah, I remember her," Erin said as offhandedly as she could. "Is she back in town?"

"No, the British Interpol office sent this," Vic said. "Since we've got a warrant outstanding for her, they let us know if anything pops on their side. Looks like she shot some guys in Belfast last week."

"Really? What guys?"

"Three suspected UVF terrorists," he said, referring to the Ulster Volunteer Front, an anti-IRA paramilitary group.

"How do they know it was her?"

"According to what I got from the Brits, she walked right into the pub where these three mopes were drinking, no mask, no disguise, that long red hair of hers hanging right down her back, pulled a pistol, said something to get their attention, wasted all three of them, dropped a ten-pound note on the table to pay for their beer, and walked out again."

"What'd she say?"

"No one heard it clearly enough."

"Witnesses?"

"Plenty. Half a dozen statements, all pretty much agreeing. Plus, they got the banknote; they'll be able to get DNA off it. She didn't care they knew it was her."

"Sounds like an IRA job," she said.

Vic shook his head. "If it was, they had buyer's remorse. Sinn Fein, the IRA political boys, immediately denied responsibility. They've disavowed her. You know, like in *Mission: Impossible*?"

"You saying Siobhan's a secret agent now?"

"No, I'm saying she's gone off the reservation. She's a crazy free agent. The IRA must be shitting bricks right now, wondering what else she's gonna do."

"I'll say," Erin said quietly. An uneasy peace had held in Northern Ireland ever since the Good Friday Accords had ostensibly put an end to the decades-long low-grade civil war the Irish called The Troubles. A rogue operative knocking off members of the other side would be just the thing that could restart the cycle of killings, bombings, and terrorism.

"Not that we can do anything about that," Vic added. "Hell, the Irish want her worse than we do now. They'll be looking to scoop her up. If we want her, we'll have to wait till they're done with her, and she's looking at life, so I wouldn't hold my breath. That's if the IRA or the UVF don't get her first, in which case she'll just plain disappear."

"But they don't have her in custody?"

"You kidding? That girl's pure Teflon. We almost had her twice, but she keeps slipping through."

"Not our problem now," Erin agreed. "Nice of them to let us know. I wonder why she decided to knock off those losers?"

"Who knows? Probably one of them killed somebody on her side, who killed somebody on theirs. Isn't that how that whole thing worked for about five hundred years?"

"Pretty much," she sighed.

"Tell you what," he said. "I'll send you the Interpol file, just for giggles."

"What's funny?" asked a familiar voice from the stairwell.

"Nothing, sir," Erin said as Lieutenant Webb walked in. Rolf's nostrils twitched as Erin's commanding officer walked past her desk. Fresh cigarette smoke wafted off his old trench coat. He'd been grabbing a smoke break outside.

"Good," Webb said. "You two look bored. Want some excitement?"

Vic perked up visibly. "We catch a body?"

"That's right. Normally this one would go to Homicide, but those boys have three detectives down with some stomach bug, so I told Lieutenant Peterson we'd pick up the slack. Sounds like one of the Homicide guys had a bachelor party and he and his buddies got a bad batch of oysters."

"Serves 'em right," Vic said. "It's a little late in the season for oysters."

"So we've got a garden-variety homicide?" Erin asked.

"One victim, female, apparent assault and murder. Duane Street, upstairs apartment. Just happened this morning. The scene's at least three hours old. Let's not let it get any colder than it already is."

Erin and Vic got up. Rolf sprang up from his snoozing spot next to Erin's desk, ready for action.

"We got a dead person," Vic said. "The day's only getting better."

"Not for her, it isn't," Erin said.

"Killjoy," he said. "You know you love this shit, admit it."

"What do you know about love?" she shot back.

"I've heard it's all around, but CSU never seems to find it at our crime scenes."

"No love at murder scenes? Gee, I wonder why."

Chapter 2

Webb was right. The crime scene wasn't exactly fresh. A bored-looking Patrol officer was standing guard at the apartment, but the paramedics had come and gone. The site of the crime was a second-floor unit in a four-story apartment with the ironic name of the Hope Building.

"I guess this is the place," Vic said, cocking his head at the door of Unit 202. "If I had to, I'd guess there's signs of foul play."

The uniformed officer gave him a lopsided smile. "You could say that." The door stood open. Even a quick glance showed splintered wood around the doorframe. Bits of broken wood were strewn across the carpet.

"Where's the victim?" Webb asked.

"Hospital morgue," the cop said. "The responding officer thought there might be a chance to save her. The EMTs took her to Bellevue, but I heard she was DOA."

"I'll call the hospital," Erin said. Her brother was a trauma surgeon at Bellevue and would be glad to tell her what was going on.

"No rush on that," Webb said. "The body will keep. Let's take a look around."

"The scene will be contaminated," Vic predicted.

"Of course it will," Webb said. "That's what happens when the medics get there first. Deal with it."

"Where's CSU?" Erin asked.

"They'll be here soon," he replied.

"Who was the victim?" Vic asked.

"Amelia Bledsoe's the name on the lease," Webb said.

Erin pulled on a pair of disposable gloves and peered into the apartment. Just inside, a claw hammer lay on the floor. She knelt beside it and looked closely, but didn't touch it.

"No blood," she reported. "Looks like it was used to pry open the door, but the perp dropped it once he got inside."

"Wonder why," Vic said. "A hammer's a pretty handy weapon." He turned to the uniformed officer. "What killed her?"

"EMTs said it was strangulation. She had something wrapped around her neck."

Erin, Vic, and Webb shared a look. All of them were thinking the same thing. Vic was the one who said it.

"Sounds like a sex crime."

Erin nodded. Strangling someone was a tricky business and a robber wouldn't have bothered when he could just bash the victim's head in. Strangling the victim was a personal, intimate gesture.

"Any signs of sexual assault?" Webb asked.

The cop shrugged. "Dunno."

"We'll know that at the autopsy," Erin said. "Can we get Levine on it?"

Sarah Levine was Precinct 8's Medical Examiner. She was a little strange, but very good at her job.

"Sure thing," Webb said. "It's our case, so our people. I'll let her know, have her go to the hospital to pick up the body."

"Where was she found?" Erin asked the cop.

"Bedroom."

"Of course," Vic muttered. "I'm telling you, sex crime."

The detectives made their way through the apartment. It was comfortably furnished, but didn't look like a particularly wealthy residence. They passed the living room, where the bookshelves had been swept clean. Books, mostly trade paperbacks, were scattered everywhere. A lamp had been knocked over and lay across the detritus.

"Someone looking for something," Vic guessed.

"Maybe," Webb said doubtfully. "Not much of a ransacking."

"Who else lives here?" Erin asked.

"I saw a pair of men's dress shoes by the front door," Vic said. "A guy lives here for sure. I don't think kids."

Erin nodded. Her brother Sean had two children, aged eight and six, which was immediately obvious upon entering their house.

"Small mercies," Webb said, poking open the bathroom door. "I hate when kids are involved. Nothing out of place in here."

"Not junkies, then," Erin said. Addicts looking for a fix always went for the medicine cabinets.

"It'll be a pervert," Vic predicted. "Some rapist asshole who just graduated to murder."

"It better not be," Erin said, and Webb nodded agreement. All of them knew sex crimes were some of the most likely violent crimes to be repeated. If their perp got a taste for it, they could be looking at a budding serial killer.

Webb got to the bedroom door first. He stopped in the doorway.

"Well?" Vic said, craning his neck to peer over his boss's shoulder.

"I'd say we've got signs of a struggle," Webb said dryly, stepping gingerly into the room.

It wasn't a very large room, but it looked like a tornado had torn through the place. There were two dressers. One appeared intact, but every drawer had been pulled out of the other one and its contents upended across the carpet. The bedclothes were pulled and torn, sheets and comforter in a crumpled mass. A few framed photos, which Erin guessed had been on top of the dresser, were lying next to it in a sparkling pile of broken glass.

It was impossible to tell what had happened. The EMTs, in their well-intentioned attempt to save the victim's life, had hopelessly contaminated the scene, as Vic had predicted.

"Hey!" Vic called back to the uniformed cop, who had taken up his old position at the entrance.

"Yeah?"

"Was she on the bed, or what?"

"Yeah, she was lying there, right in the middle of the bed, arms and legs all spread out."

"What was she wearing?" Erin asked.

"One of them, you know, robe things."

"A bathrobe?"

"Yeah, the fuzzy kind. Pink. The belt was pulled off it. That was the thing around her neck."

"Choked her with her own bathrobe," Webb said.

"That's a bad way to go," Vic said.

"You find a good way, let me know," Webb said.

"Was the robe open or closed?" Erin asked.

The cop didn't answer. He cleared his throat and looked uncomfortable.

"I asked you a question, Officer," Erin said sharply.

"It was open," he said quietly.

"Was she wearing anything else? Under it?"

"Yeah. Underwear."

"Bra and panties, both?"

"No, just the bottom part."

"If she was still wearing her underwear, she may not have been raped," Webb said thoughtfully. "That may make it harder to get DNA."

Erin swallowed an angry response. She hoped the victim hadn't been raped as well as murdered, for reasons of common humanity. But Webb did have a point. If the attacker had left any body fluids on his victim, it would make a conviction a slam-dunk if they could catch the guy.

She looked around the room, looking for patterns, for anything that would make sense. Rolf stood at her side, waiting for instructions. Unfortunately, there wasn't much for him to do right now. His specialties were tracking and suspect apprehension, with a sideline in explosives detection, and there was no need for those skills at the moment.

"It's the woman's dresser," she said.

"What's that?" Webb asked.

"The clothes," she said, gesturing to the heaps around the room. "The attacker dumped all her drawers. He didn't touch the other one."

Vic went to the other dresser and opened one of the drawers. "You're right," he said. "This one's full of men's clothing. Untouched. Maybe our guy's got a thing for women's underwear. You know, gets off on going through their stuff."

"Or taking trophies," she said. Her skin was crawling. This was looking more and more like a serial killer. It wouldn't be the first one for her; she'd taken down a serial murderer last year. It hadn't been a pleasant experience, especially once he'd picked her for his next victim.

"That's speculation," Webb said. "I don't know what else we can see here, but Neshenko and I will keep looking. I want you at the hospital, O'Reilly. Connect with Levine, see what you can find out about the manner of death. We'll see what more we can learn about her."

"And her husband, or boyfriend, or whatever," Vic added. "Hell, he probably doesn't even know she's dead yet."

"Copy that," Erin said. She twitched the leash and gave her K-9 a command in his native German. "Rolf, *komm!* We're going to see my brother."

*   *   *

"Erin, how many times do I have to tell you, I don't want you in my emergency room?" Sean O'Reilly Junior said in mock exasperation.

"I'm not coming in on a stretcher, so you don't get to complain," she replied with a smile. "How's it going, Junior?" She moved in for a quick hug with her oldest brother. "Busy day?"

"Not too bad. Better than nighttime and weekend shifts." He gestured around the almost-empty ER of Bellevue Hospital. "I just got done with an emergency appendectomy. Pretty routine. You're here about that young woman they brought in this morning?"

"Yeah. Were you the one who worked on her?"

"If you can call it that." Sean sighed and ran a hand through his hair. "Wasn't much I could do. She was brought in without a pulse or respiration. We gave it our best shot, but it was just so we could look her next of kin in the eye and tell them we did everything we could."

Erin squeezed his arm. "Sorry."

"Comes with the territory," he said. "I knew that sort of thing would happen when I went into trauma medicine. You just try to focus on the ones you do save. It's the ones I could've saved that keep me up nights. That girl was dead before she got here."

"You got her downstairs, in the morgue?"

"Yeah. Someone from the Medical Examiner got here a little ahead of you."

"Doctor Levine?"

"I think so, yeah. Female, dark hair, poor social skills?"

"That's her," Erin said.

"Where's Rolf?" he asked.

"I left him in the car with the air conditioner running. He'll be bored, but it'll keep him out of the way. Anything else you can tell me about our victim?"

"Just that whoever killed her wanted to hurt her. It looked like she'd been beaten pretty badly around the face and upper body. But the ME will be able to tell you at least as much about that as I can. I wish I didn't recognize it, but we get lots of abuse and assault victims through here."

"And she didn't say anything?"

"No, like I said, she was nonresponsive when she got here. The medics had been trying to resuscitate her in the ambulance, but they didn't get anything either. Have you notified next of kin?"

"Not yet. Has anyone been by?"

"No. We didn't even have a name when she came in. No ID on her."

"We think she's Amelia Bledsoe," Erin said. "But we'll need to confirm it."

"Then you know more about her than I do. Good luck, sis."

"You too."

"Say, Erin, you're still coming by for dinner, aren't you?"

"Yeah, I think so."

"Great. Shelley's been experimenting out of that gourmet cookbook I got her last Christmas."

"So you're saying I should eat something before coming over?"

"I'm going to tell her you said that."

"You wouldn't!" Erin swatted him on the shoulder.

"See you at seven," he said, smiling.

* * *

The hospital morgue was all cold fluorescent light, stainless steel, and dreary tile. Erin wished she had brought Rolf with her; the energetic K-9 would have helped counteract the sense of icy death that hung around the place.

She found Doctor Levine standing beside a cooling slab, upon which lay their victim. Levine was examining the body's hands.

"Hey, Doc," Erin said. "Find anything out yet?"

Levine didn't look up from her examination. She spoke in a distracted, almost expressionless voice. "Female Caucasian, age mid-twenties, sixty-five inches in height, weight approximately one hundred forty pounds. Preliminary cause of death, judging from eight-ball hemorrhage in the eyes and ligature marks on the throat, was asphyxiation due to strangulation. Time of death was approximately 8:45 this morning. The body shows secondary wounds consistent with a close-quarters struggle."

"Did she get some hits in on her attacker?" Erin asked.

"I'm examining her hands now," Levine said, a hint of impatience coming into her tone. "I'll need to take scrapings under the fingernails to try to find skin cells. She does have defensive wounds on her hands and forearms, so she apparently tried to defend herself."

"Any signs of sexual assault?"

"I'll need to make a closer examination to be certain," Levine said. "However, I see no outward indicator."

"The secondary wounds," Erin said, forcing herself to look at the body as dispassionately as she could. Amelia Bledsoe was a fairly pretty young woman, once she looked past the swelling and contusions on her face and, of course, the eerie dark purple eyes that stared sightlessly back at her. Levine was right, that was a characteristic of victims who had been strangled. Blood vessels in the eyes burst, resulting in the eight-ball hemorrhage phenomenon. She'd seen it in people who had survived attacks as well. Her old Field Training Officer said living people with eyes like that had "Lazarus eyes," referencing the dead man Jesus had revived.

"What about them?" Levine asked.

"Do you know what made them? What kind of weapon?"

"The bruise patterning is consistent with a bare-handed attack. I see no marks that would indicate a weapon."

"The officer on scene said the victim was strangled with the belt from her bathrobe," Erin said.

"That is consistent with the ligature marks," Levine said, pointing. "The stippling effect on the skin would be a match for terrycloth."

"You know what a terrycloth strangulation looks like?" Erin asked in slightly horrified fascination.

"I've examined a large number of fabrics for their utility in binding and strangulation," Levine said matter-of-factly.

"Oh. Good."

There was an awkward pause.

"Will you be taking the body back to the Eightball?" Erin asked, recovering.

"Yes, I'll want to perform the autopsy at the Eight. I'll run the bloodwork there as well. Transport is on the way now."

"You mean Hank and Ernie?"

Levine made no response. It didn't matter to her. But Erin had no desire to be there when the guys from the Coroner's Office arrived driving what they called the Meat Wagon.

"Let us know what you find out," she said and started for the door.

She almost made it. But she was still a few feet short of the exit when she heard the rattle of a gurney on its way down the hall. A moment later, the door swung open and Hank and Ernie pushed their cart into the room.

It wasn't that they were bad guys, exactly, though they did remind her uncomfortably of Horace and Jasper, the dim-witted henchmen in *One Hundred and One Dalmatians*. Ernie was tall and thin, with a long nose. Hank was short and fat. They survived their job, collecting the dead from crime scenes and accident sites, on a diet of junk food and pitch-black humor. Erin found them annoying at the best of times.

"Afternoon, Detective," Ernie said, putting a hand to his forehead as if tipping a nonexistent hat. "Where's the dear departed?"

Erin poked a thumb over her shoulder and said nothing. She didn't want to encourage them.

"What killed her?" Hank asked.

"I heard, asphyxiation," Ernie said. Erin had no idea how he managed to get that information ahead of time. Maybe he talked to ghosts. She wouldn't bet against it.

"Maybe she was listening to your wife," Hank said. "At one of her afternoon parties. All the air just got sucked out of the room."

As Erin sidled around them and got out of there, she heard Ernie starting to sing an oldie song.

"Turning and returning to some secret place inside. Watching in slow motion as you turn around and say..."

Hank joined in for the chorus. *"Take my breath away..."*

"Thanks, guys," she muttered under her breath. "Now I'll never be able to watch *Top Gun* again."

Chapter 3

Erin successfully steered clear of the coroner's van on the way back to the Eightball. She was thinking about her last experience with a serial killer, remembering what she'd learned. The Heartbreaker Killer, as the newspapers had called him, had been a very methodical, organized murderer. He'd chosen his victims carefully, stalked them, and killed them in an extremely planned and precise way. They'd gotten him by playing on those tendencies, drawing him into a trap.

That wouldn't work here. This case's MO was totally different. The Heartbreaker Killer had gone to great lengths to leave the scenes undisturbed. That had been one of the eeriest things about him; the locked-room mystery component. He'd been so effective that several of his early kills had been mislabeled as suicides. Amelia Bledsoe's murderer had been in some kind of frenzy. The way he'd broken down the door, thrown away the tool he'd used to break in, and then smashed and tossed the contents of the apartment showed a strong emotional component to his attack.

Erin didn't know for sure that the murderer was male, but she was making an assumption on the basis of statistics. Most murderers were men, and almost all violent home invasions and murders of women were committed by men. Also, ninety percent of serial killers were male.

"That's four million suspects ruled out," she told Rolf.

Rolf smiled at her, letting his tongue hang out. It sounded like good news to him.

"We need to know if this was random, or a planned attack," she said. She liked bouncing ideas off her partner. He didn't contribute much, but he was a great listener. "If it was a random break-in, we're screwed. But if he stalked her ahead of time, someone may have seen him."

Rolf kept listening, waiting for her to get to the part where they chased the bad guys. That was his favorite part of every case.

"The apartment didn't have cameras," she added. She'd looked in the lobby on the way out. "Maybe we'll get lucky and Bledsoe had a nosy neighbor." The timeline was a little iffy. Most people would have left for work, but all it took was one person who'd been in the right place at the right time.

Erin sighed. They were still at the part of the case where they were tugging on everything, seeing what might pull a clue loose and give them the break they needed.

She parked in the precinct garage and hurried upstairs to Major Crimes, Rolf trotting beside her. She found Vic sitting at his computer.

"Where's the Lieutenant?" she asked.

"Still at the scene," he replied. "Interviewing neighbors."

"Who called it in?"

"Woman who lives down the hall. She was taking her laundry out and saw the door busted in."

"Did she go inside?"

"No. She told the responding officer she'd seen too many thrillers. She knows what happens when you poke your head in; the killer's always waiting for you."

Erin looked at the department's whiteboard. Vic had filled in the beginnings of a timeline, starting with the 911 call at 9:25. She added Levine's estimate which put the time of death at 8:45.

"Anything interesting from the hospital?" Vic asked.

"Nothing we didn't already know. She was beaten and strangled. Levine thinks it was a barehanded attack."

"That's weird," Vic said. "The guy had this perfectly good hammer right there."

"You're fixated on that hammer."

"If I want to kill someone, I'm using a weapon to do it. That's all I'm saying."

"But you don't get your sick thrills by killing."

"No, I get my sick thrills other ways. But you're right. It's probably what gets him off, choking his victims. Perverted bastard. I wouldn't mind getting my hands on his neck for a couple minutes. That might give me a thrill."

"I was thinking in the car," Erin said.

"You shouldn't do that," he said. "Distracted driving is dangerous."

"That scene seemed pretty disorganized," she said, ignoring him.

"Well, yeah. It was a break-in and murder. Those are messy."

"The damage was haphazard," she said. "Books on the floor, and that lamp. Why knock over the lamp? It's not like that was hiding anything. And only turning out her dresser, not his?"

"What're you getting at, Erin? You think he was coked up, maybe? Or just plain crazy?"

"Maybe." But she wasn't sure. All she knew was that something felt weird about the scene. Something didn't quite fit, but she couldn't put her finger on it.

Both of them paused and looked toward the stairwell. A man had just climbed the stairs and was standing in the doorway. Erin instantly pegged him as a civilian; he was dressed in slacks and a red polo shirt with a small company logo over the breast pocket, and was a little too carefully groomed and preppy to be either a cop or any of the usual precinct denizens. He looked agitated, like a Ralph Lauren model who needed a drug fix. He had his hands in his pockets and a nervous, excited look on his face.

"Help you?" Vic grunted.

"I need to talk to someone. The guy at the desk downstairs told me to come up here. I'm looking for a Lieutenant Webb, or Webster, or something."

"Lieutenant Webb is out," Erin said. "I'm his second in command. Detective O'Reilly. What can I do for you?"

"I'm looking for my wife."

"You can file a missing persons report at the front desk—" Vic began, but Erin interrupted.

"What's your name, sir?" she asked.

"Ryan Bledsoe."

There was a brief silence. Vic and Erin exchanged a look.

"What's your wife's name?" Erin asked.

"Amelia. I called her over my lunch break, just checking in, and a policeman answered. He said my wife wasn't there, that she'd been taken to the hospital. But he didn't know which one. I called four hospitals, but none of them had her listed as a patient. One of them eventually transferred me back to the police. Now, do you know where my wife is or not?"

"Mr. Bledsoe," Erin said, "come sit down for a moment."

"What? Why? I'm not going to sit down! I demand you tell me where my wife is!"

Vic got to his feet as Bledsoe took several steps toward Erin. "Take it easy, buddy," he said.

Erin decided the best thing was to just say it. "Mr. Bledsoe, it appears your apartment was broken into this morning. Your wife was attacked by the intruder. I'm sorry, but she was killed."

Bledsoe stopped his advance. "Wait, what? What did you say?"

"Amelia was taken to Bellevue Hospital, where she was pronounced dead on arrival," Erin said as gently as she could.

"No. No, that's not right. There has to be some mistake. Have you talked to the hospital?"

"I was just there, sir."

"No!" he shouted. He took the last couple of steps to Erin's desk and banged his fists down on the desktop. "No!"

"Easy," Vic said again, closing on Bledsoe from the right. He didn't want to get in a fight, but he obviously didn't intend to let even a grief-stricken husband go out of control.

"How could she do this to me?" Bledsoe shouted.

Erin blinked. "Sir, I don't know if I've made myself clear. Your wife has been murdered. This wasn't something she did to herself."

"How could she leave me like this?" Bledsoe brought down his fists again with a bang. Rolf was on his feet, bristling at the man, a low growl rising in his chest. He didn't like angry people standing so close to his partner. Vic was on the other side of him, also poised for action in case things got ugly.

Erin remained seated, trying to stay calm. She reminded herself that this man had been catapulted into a nightmare. Police work all too often involved meeting people on the worst days of their lives. You couldn't expect them to be calm and rational. This poor guy had hit the desk so hard he'd damaged his hands. He was actually bleeding slightly. There was blood on her desk.

"Sir, I'm sorry," she said. "I promise you, we'll do everything we can to find the person who did this. And to do that, we need you to help us. Were you at your apartment this morning?"

Bledsoe paused. "Huh? Oh, yeah. Yeah, of course I was. I live there."

"Where did you go?"

"To work. I'm the floor manager at the Quick-Mart on West Broadway."

"When did you leave for work?"

"A little after 8:30."

Vic and Erin exchanged another quick look. He must have missed the intruder by bare minutes.

"Did you see anyone suspicious hanging around the apartment, either inside or just outside?" Erin asked.

He shook his head. "No. No, I don't think... oh, wait."

Erin felt a surge of excitement. "What?" she asked. "Whatever you can remember may help."

"Yeah, there was this one guy. A black guy, in a gray hoodie. He was in the lobby, with his hands in his pockets."

"Did you get a look at his face?" she asked.

"Not a great one. He had the hood up."

"Would you recognize him if you saw him again?" Vic asked.

"Yeah, I think so."

"Have you seen this man before?" Erin asked.

"Uh, maybe. I think maybe I've seen him hanging around some mornings."

"Always in the lobby?"

"Yeah. You think he's the guy who... who did that... to my wife?"

"That's what we're trying to find out," Erin said. "How tall would you say this man was?"

"About my height."

"Heavier or lighter than you?"

"A little bigger." Bledsoe wasn't heavily built.

"Could you see his hair?"

"No. I think his head was shaved, maybe."

"What kind of pants was he wearing?"

"Blue jeans, I think. Yeah, blue jeans."

"Shoes?"

"Shoes? I have no idea. I don't usually look at a guy's feet."

"Did he have any distinguishing marks? Scars, tattoos, anything like that?"

Bledsoe shook his head. "No, he was kind of a pretty boy. Real smooth skin, kind of feminine looking."

"Feminine how?" Erin asked.

"I don't know. Just... soft. Oh, he had an earring."

"Just one? In one ear?"

"Yeah. It was gold, kind of a funky shape."

"Thank you," Erin said. She was noting down everything he'd said. "That's a big help. Here's one of my cards, in case you remember anything else. You can call me anytime."

He took the card. "Thanks. I want to see her now."

"We'll need you to confirm her identity," Erin said. "Just a moment; I'll just call the coroner and get things ready for you."

"Where's the coroner?" he demanded. "I'm going down there now."

"That's not a good idea, buddy," Vic said. He put a hand on Bledsoe's shoulder.

The other man shrugged him angrily off. "Don't 'buddy' me, jerkoff! And don't tell me what I can't do! This is my wife we're talking about, and I want to see her right now!"

"Sir, you don't want to see her like this," Erin said. "We just need a chance to get her ready. It'll be better to remember her that way. Please, trust us. This is what we do."

Bledsoe fumed, but nodded. "Okay, make your damn phone call."

Erin called the morgue.

Levine answered. "Morgue."

"Hey, Levine, this is Erin O'Reilly. We've got Amelia Bledsoe's husband here. He's ready to do the identification."

"I'm still performing the external examination, planning to move to the Y incision once I finish."

"Good. Don't start. Please move her to the gallery. How long will that take?"

"Ten minutes."

"Okay, we'll be down then. Thanks." Erin hung up and turned to Bledsoe. "They'll be ready for us in ten minutes. There's a coffee machine in the break room over there. I can give you the contact information for a grief counselor. We have people whose job it is to help people in your situation."

"Yeah, coffee sounds good," Bledsoe said. He disappeared into the break room.

"Real ray of sunshine," Vic said in a very quiet undertone.

"Give him a pass," Erin whispered. "He just lost his wife."

He nodded and updated the whiteboard with Ryan Bledsoe's departure from the apartment. Then they waited. Ten minutes was just long enough for everyone to get good and uncomfortable, but not long enough to get any useful work done. All three were visibly glad to go downstairs, even though it wasn't a pleasant task that was waiting for them.

The viewing gallery was a plain, dark room with a full-length window on one side that overlooked a metal table. On the table lay the body of the victim, covered from the neck down. Levine stood next to the table.

"Please take your time," Erin said to Bledsoe. "Take as long as you need."

"That's her," he said in a low, trembling voice. "Yeah, that's my wife."

"I'm sorry," she said.

"How do I get my hands on her? I mean, her... body."

Erin was ready for the clumsily-worded question. She gave him another card with the name and phone number of the NYPD's family-assistance contact. "She'll help you with this," she said. "Give her a call. She'll let you know what you need to do."

"Okay. Sorry I yelled at you earlier," he said quietly.

"Forget about it," she said. "It's okay."

"We'll need your phone number," Vic said. "In case we need to contact you again. You got somewhere you can stay?"

"I have a home," he said. Then he paused. "Oh. Right. I guess I can't stay there right now."

"We'll release the scene as soon as we can," Erin said. "In the meantime, do you have family in the area?"

"I'll be okay," he said. "I'd like to get some of my stuff out of the apartment. Clothes and things."

"We'll have an officer get them for you," she said.

*   *   *

Lieutenant Webb arrived at the precinct shortly after Ryan Bledsoe had left. Erin wondered whether it was dumb luck, or some veteran police instinct, that had allowed him to narrowly miss having to deal with the widower. Webb really didn't like the emotional side of the Job.

"CSU is still going over the apartment," he said. "But they already found one useful thing."

"Fingerprints?" Erin guessed.

"Blood sample?" Vic suggested.

Webb shook his head and produced an evidence bag. In it was a Smartphone.

"The victim's?" Erin asked.

"Yeah," he said.

"What good does that do us?" Vic asked. "I mean, it's not like she snapped a picture of her attacker."

"We don't know that," Webb said. "And it's only a guess that she didn't know her killer. Let's dump the phone and see what she was up to."

"Yeah," Vic said. "Suppose she meets this guy online, say, and they do some texting, she sends him some nude pics, maybe they go on a date, it turns out he's a psycho stalker."

"You're wasted in Major Crimes," Erin said. "You should talk to Tad Brown in Vice. He's always looking for kindred spirits."

"I'm depressed enough without that sad bastard dragging me down," he replied.

"I don't know about that," she said. "From what I've seen, he's actually pretty happy with his job."

"That's even more depressing."

Webb was hooking up the phone to his computer while Erin and Vic bantered. He turned it on and blinked in surprise.

"It's not secured," he said.

"That's not smart," Vic observed. "Any old jerk can get at your data that way. I want a look." He and Erin hurried over to Webb's desk and looked over his shoulder as he downloaded the phone's contents.

"Okay, let's see what we've got," Webb said. "We'll start with call history. Hmm, nothing today, got a call yesterday from an unknown number."

"Telemarketer, maybe," Vic said.

"Or the killer," Erin said.

"It's not the first call from that number," Webb said. "It's all over her call history. If it's a friend, I wonder why they're not in her contact list."

"We could call them and find out," Vic said.

"I wouldn't," Erin said. "If it's the killer, it could spook them."

Webb nodded. "Maybe later," he said thoughtfully. "Let's try her text messages. Oh... what's this? Message chain from the same phone number. Looks like a continuation of a previous conversation. See how it starts? This person's answering a question she asked earlier. She must have deleted the previous texts."

Erin nodded. As she examined the text chain, she felt a chill. Whatever this conversation was, it had to be connected to the murder.

I can't see you today.

Why not?

I can't see you anymore. We can't keep doing this.

Doing what? We're not doing anything wrong.

I'm scared.

I'm sorry. I never meant you to get hurt. I just wanted to help.

Please, don't make this hard.

You're my friend, Amelia. I want to do something. Let me.

Okay. Sometimes I think you're the only one who understands me.

Thanks. You know I love you.

Love you too, man.

"You know I love you," Vic repeated.

"I wonder what Ryan would say about this," Erin said.

"It'd be nice if she said this guy's name," Webb said. "Or anything about him."

"Let's ping his phone," Erin suggested.

"Good idea," Webb said. "And we'll clone Amelia's phone, in case he sends anything. Then we can reel him in. I'll get the warrant to access this guy's GPS location."

Obtaining the warrant took about an hour, which wasn't bad as such things went. The detectives filled up the time with some of the giant stack of paperwork a homicide investigation entailed. Erin also looked up Ryan Bledsoe's place of work and called it.

"Quick-Mart, this is Marty," said the guy who answered the phone.

"Marty... at Quick-Mart," she repeated.

"Yeah, I know, I know," he said wearily. The strangeness of the name was new to Erin, but not new to Marty at all. "What can I do for you, ma'am?"

"This is Detective O'Reilly, NYPD Major Crimes. Are you the manager?"

"Wait a sec. Is this some kind of joke?"

"No, sir."

"Um, yes. I'm the manager."

"What's your full name, please?"

"Martin Pohl. That's P-O-H-L."

"Does a Ryan Bledsoe work there?"

"Yeah, he's the floor manager, that means he's usually the guy out front, but he's not here. He went on his lunch break and then said he was taking the rest of the day off. That's why I'm answering the phone. I'm the only guy here, so can we keep this short? I got customers."

"I just need to know when Mr. Bledsoe arrived at work today."

"Huh? Well, he opened the store at nine."

"Was anyone else there at the time?"

"No. I came in at noon."

"How do you know he opened at nine?"

There was a short pause. "We clock in on the store computer. Just a sec. Ryan clocked in at... let's see, 9:02. A couple minutes late I guess. What's going on?"

"I'm not at liberty to discuss it, sir. Thanks for your cooperation." Erin hung up and added that information to the board.

The warrant came through on the department's ancient fax machine. Erin figured fax machines were like VCRs. No one made any new ones, and the old ones just sat around slowly turning yellow and dusty. Webb retrieved the document and promptly called the phone company. After going a few rounds with the company's bureaucrats, he hung up his phone triumphantly.

"We've got a location," he said. "The phone's turned on and the GPS is engaged."

That was good news. Using cell-tower triangulation would have gotten them within about three-quarters of a mile. The GPS on a Smartphone would get them within sixteen feet; that would put them practically in the same room with their target.

"Awesome," Vic said, jumping to his feet. Erin and Rolf were right behind him. "What's the address?"

"1071 Fifth Avenue," Webb reported.

"I know that address," Vic said. "Hold on, it'll come to me. Oh, right! It's the Guggenheim."

"Unbelievable," Erin said.

"Hey, murderers go to museums, too," Vic said.

"No, it's unbelievable that you recognize the address of an art museum."

"Bite me, O'Reilly. I got plenty of culture. I got culture coming out my ears."

"It's funny, Vic. When you say 'culture,' I hear 'bullshit.'"

"Knock it off," Webb said. "Let's roll, people. We'll get another ping from the phone company once we're on site, just in case he's moved."

"The Guggenheim's that building that looks like a space station, right?" Erin said.

"And you complain about me," Vic snorted. "I've actually been inside. I think the architect was on drugs when he built it."

"The architect was Frank Lloyd Wright," Webb said. "He's one of the most respected architects in America."

"Definitely on drugs," Vic said.

Chapter 4

Vic was right, the Guggenheim museum looked weird. It was white, all curves, with the main building rising up and out as if a giant drill bit had been screwed partway into Fifth Avenue. The detectives couldn't help taking a moment to stand outside and stare at it.

"It's art, isn't it," Vic said. "The building, I mean."

"I guess," Erin said. "What makes it art?"

"I think if you can't understand it, it's modern art," he replied.

Webb was already connected with the phone company. "Our guy's still inside," he reported. "He's somewhere in that spiral, but unfortunately, GPS can't judge altitude, so he could be on any floor."

"Sir, how do we find him?" Erin asked. "We don't know what he looks like. There's probably hundreds of people in there."

Webb rubbed his chin. "We'll split up," he said. "The gallery is a spiral that's open in the middle. With the three of us, we'll be able to see most of it. Once we're in position, I'll call him on the cloned phone. Keep your eyes open for anyone answering a call."

"There's gonna be three dozen teenage girls all staring at their phones," Vic predicted.

"And look for a man, probably an African-American guy about Ryan Bledsoe's height," Erin said. "Shaved head, maybe a gold earring."

"That narrows it down," Webb said. "That's the best we can do. I'll try to get the guy to identify himself. Watch for anyone who spooks, especially if they throw away the phone or run for the exit."

"He won't make it if he tries," Erin said, patting Rolf. No human on earth could outrun a German Shepherd.

They showed their shields to the people at the door, who let them in. They'd agreed that Vic would take the top position, Webb the middle, and Erin the lowest. That was because Webb was in the worst shape, so didn't want to climb all the way up the gallery, but Erin and Rolf needed to be ready to cut off their target's retreat if he did make a run for it. Accordingly, Erin loitered on the second loop of the gigantic spiral.

The last time Erin had been in an art museum had been down in Queens, after she'd helped retrieve a lost Renaissance painting. She'd be the first to admit that she didn't have much appreciation for fine art. Now she ignored the exhibits altogether and concentrated on the patrons. She saw all kinds of New Yorkers, all shapes, sizes, colors, and sexes. As Vic had said, she also saw an awful lot of people staring at their phones. Picking out one person wasn't going to be easy.

Her own phone buzzed with a text from Vic, confirming he was in position. Webb sent a reply that read "10 seconds." She counted down in her head and scanned the crowd, both around her and across the way.

Directly opposite her, three guys who looked like museum employees were looking at a patch of wall and discussing something. One of them, a Black guy with a shaved head, suddenly paused and reached into his hip pocket. He pulled out a phone and put it to his ear.

Erin started moving. She couldn't call Webb, since he was on the phone, but she speed-dialed Vic. As his phone rang, she threaded her way through startled art patrons, Rolf weaving between bodies.

"Got something?" Vic asked by way of greeting.

"Yeah. One floor up, Black guy, shaved head, white shirt, khaki slacks."

"On my way," he said.

Erin shoved her phone back in her pocket. Her path was blocked by a junior high class and their teacher, who was lecturing them on a painting. She whipped out her shield.

"NYPD! Coming through!" she snapped.

The kids just stared at her.

"Move it, kiddos," she said, waving her hand.

"Whoa, cool," said a twelve-year-old boy. But they made a hole and she went through it.

For a second she lost her target, but then she saw him again. He was still holding his phone to his ear, and was about thirty yards from her. Just then, he turned toward her and they made eye contact. His eyes got wide when he saw her running toward him, accompanied by a ninety-pound German Shepherd.

"NYPD!" she said again. "Stop right there! Hands where I can see them!" She pulled out her Glock and held it at her hip, ready to bring it in line.

She saw the sudden fear in his face. He dropped the phone. It hit the floor in a splinter of broken plastic. He put his hands up. The people around him were frozen in shock, all of them watching Erin's approach.

"Keep those hands up!" she ordered, closing to about ten feet.

"Lady, there's some sort of mistake," he said in a deep, quiet voice. "I haven't done anything."

"Amelia Bledsoe," she said, watching him closely. He was a good-looking man, probably in his mid-twenties. He had a gold earring in his right ear.

She saw the recognition of the name in his eyes, but she'd been hoping for something more. Guilt, maybe. Better yet, he could have run. He wouldn't have gotten far. Rolf would have been on him before he could make it ten steps.

"Hey, lady, leave the guy alone!" someone shouted just behind Erin. "He didn't do nothing!"

"What's your name?" she demanded.

"Curtis Dahl, ma'am. I work here. I didn't do anything."

"I'm going to need you to come with me, Curtis," she said, holstering her gun.

"Am I under arrest?"

"Only if you resist."

"I'm not going to resist."

Vic came charging down the spiral, Webb puffing in his wake. He looked disappointed when he found Erin standing in front of a quiet, polite man who was offering no trouble.

"This our guy?" he asked.

"There's been a mistake," Dahl repeated.

"Then we'll sort it out at the station," Erin said.

*   *   *

Erin expected Curtis Dahl to lawyer up immediately, but he didn't. He flinched a little when she put the cuffs on him, but made no other resistance. Vic put him in the back of his Taurus and drove him and Webb back to the precinct, Erin tailing them with Rolf in her Charger. They booked him and put him in an interrogation room, then conferred in the observation room next door.

"I like him for this," Webb said. "I'll take the lead. O'Reilly, you're with me."

"What am I, the dog sitter?" Vic asked.

"Exactly," Erin said. "Rolf, *sitz. Bleib.* If Vic moves, you have my permission to eat him."

Rolf settled himself next to Vic and gave him a long, serious look.

"I charge by the hour," Vic said.

"Put it on the city's tab," she said. "How do you want to go at Dahl, sir?"

"This was a crime of passion," Webb said. "There was rage in it. I'm going to find his buttons, then I'm going to push those buttons as hard as I can. If we do it right, I'm betting we get a confession."

"So, you're going to be bad cop for this one? And then I come in and offer a deal once he cracks?"

"That's the idea. You ready for this, O'Reilly?"

She nodded and stepped into the hallway.

Dahl was clearly nervous, but he sat quietly on the other side of the table, watching the two detectives. Erin sat down. Webb remained standing, leaning forward across the table. Dahl drew back from him.

"You and Amelia, huh?" Webb said.

"I don't understand, sir," Dahl said.

"How long have you and she been sneaking around behind Ryan's back?" Webb snapped.

"It's not what you think," Dahl said.

"It's not what I think? You're a mind reader?" Webb leaned even further across the table. "Why don't you tell me what I'm thinking, then. Go on, I'm waiting."

Dahl stared at him, wide-eyed, and said nothing.

"This is your chance, punk," Webb said, putting a sneering edge in his voice. "Were you in love with her?"

"What? No!"

"Cut the bullshit. We've got your message history. We know what you told her."

"You can't do that! That's private! And she deleted those!" Dahl protested.

Webb smiled grimly. "How did you think we found you? We got a warrant for your phone communications. Anything on her phone, if we want it, we've got it. We know everything, pal."

Erin could see sweat forming on Dahl's forehead. He was looking increasingly frightened and flustered. Webb was definitely getting under his skin.

"If you know everything, then you know it wasn't like that," Dahl stammered. "Amelia isn't like that. She was scared, and I was helping her. As a friend."

"She was scared, huh? What was she scared of? Scared of you?" Webb demanded. He punctuated his question by banging a fist down on the metal table. Dahl jumped.

"No! She's not scared of me! I'd never hurt her! Ask her!"

Webb paused. "You want me to ask Amelia about you? When's the last time you saw her?"

"Day before yesterday," Dahl said. "We had lunch together."

"You didn't see her this morning?"

"This morning? No! What are you talking about? What's going on here?"

"I'm asking the questions, punk! Where were you from eight to nine this morning?"

"I... I... I was getting up, getting ready for work. I work at nine."

"But you made a stop at the Hope Building on the way to work."

"No! That's not on my way. I live in Yorkville. Amelia's way down south."

"Then why did a witness see you in her lobby this morning?"

"I wasn't there! Maybe there was a guy who looks like me!"

"Bullshit," Webb growled. He was right in Dahl's face now. "The same witness saw you there before, more than once. You going to tell me you've never been there? You going to lie to me about that?"

"I... sure, I've been there. A few times. But not today!"

Erin could see Dahl's composure crumbling. He looked really scared now. Webb was chipping away at him, probing for weak points in his story. The Lieutenant was good at interrogations. He had a keen eye for human weakness and was perfectly willing to be as ruthless as he had to be to exploit it. She kept waiting and listening. It wasn't quite time to throw Dahl a lifeline yet.

"Show me your hands," Webb said abruptly.

"They're right here," Dahl said, holding out his cuffed wrists.

"Turn them over."

Dahl obediently rotated his hands. Erin saw what Webb was looking for. Both of them sucked in a sharp breath.

"Your knuckles look a little beat up," Webb said in a quiet voice that managed to be more menacing than his earlier shouting. "Care to explain?"

"I prep art exhibits at the museum," Dahl said. "I was carrying up some crates from storage this morning. I banged my hand on the doorframe."

Webb snorted derisively. "You a fighting man, Mr. Dahl?"

"No!"

"You ever hit a man?"

"No!"

"You'd rather hit a woman?"

"Of course not! What are you talking about?" Dahl's eyes darted around the room. "Did someone hit Amelia? Just ask her! She'll tell you it wasn't me!"

"I can't ask her," Webb said through gritted teeth. "You don't know why, do you?"

Dahl shook his head.

"No, you wouldn't," Webb said. "Because you thought she was alive when you left her."

Dahl's eyes went even wider. "What are you talking about?" he whispered.

"She tried to break things off with you," Webb went on. "By text. And you lost it. You just flipped right out. You went to her place. You broke down the door. You tore up her apartment, you slapped her, and punched her, and choked her, and left her lying there to die. Alone."

"Amelia's... dead?"

Erin saw the tears forming in Dahl's eyes and knew it was her cue. She nudged Webb. He glanced at her and fell silent, stepping back and watching their prisoner.

She leaned in, but not as close as Webb had. "I don't think you went there meaning to hurt her," she said, keeping her tone deliberately gentle. "You did love her, I think."

"No," Dahl said softly. "No, that's not right."

"It's okay," she said. "You just wanted to talk to her. Did she refuse to open her door? That's embarrassing, humiliating. Nobody wants to be standing in the hallway like that, talking to a closed door. Maybe it was an accident. I don't think you meant her to die. You can make a deal, take a plea."

"Nonsense, O'Reilly," Webb said. "He had the hammer with him. He was planning to break in. That's premeditation, and that makes it first-degree murder."

Erin kept looking at Dahl, trying to be as earnest as possible. "My partner doesn't believe you, but I do. Just tell us what happened. You can plead down to manslaughter. I'll talk to the DA for you. I want to help you, Curtis."

Tears were rolling down Dahl's cheeks. He met Erin's eyes, though he was trembling all over. His voice shaking, he said, "I didn't kill anyone, ma'am. I didn't hurt anyone."

"We're going to have your prints on the hammer," Webb said. "And I don't care how clever you thought you were, you left evidence in that room. Everyone misses something. We'll find it, and when we do, you're going down."

Dahl bowed his head. "I think I need a lawyer, sir. I'm done talking."

Chapter 5

"Damn it!" Erin exploded, smacking her hand against the cinderblock wall in the hallway. "I thought we had him!"

"It was a good try, O'Reilly," Webb said. "I thought we had him, too."

"Solid try," Vic said, coming out of the observation room with Rolf's leash in hand. "He's tougher than he looks."

"It may not matter," Webb said. "I wasn't blowing smoke about the evidence. If we get his prints off the hammer, that's it. He's cooked."

"I'd still rather have a confession," Erin grumbled.

"How long have you been working this job, Erin?" Vic asked. "You know we got prisons chock-full of guys who didn't do it. Just ask 'em. Plenty of guys don't cop a plea."

"It'll be worse for everybody," she said. "We have to go through the trial, which will take months."

"I like testifying in court," Vic said. "Gives me an excuse to bust out my suit and tie, act all polite, scare the hell out of the lawyers."

"I don't believe you," she said.

"You're right. I hate going to court."

"Well, we can't do anything with him right now," Webb said. "He's lawyered up, which means no confession as long as he wants to keep swearing he didn't do it. It'll take CSU some time to finish dusting the apartment and collecting evidence. I'll set up a lineup for Dahl and see if we can get Mr. Bledsoe in to make an identification. If he can put Dahl at the apartment, that'll be plenty to hold him. In the meantime, I want to know everything we can find out about Dahl, especially his criminal record. I also want the Bledsoe financials. Dahl's, too, while you're at it. Start digging."

"I'll check Dahl's history," Erin volunteered. "I think it's your turn to look at the bank records, Vic."

"Lucky me," he muttered.

They moved Dahl into lockup to wait for his lawyer, then headed upstairs to begin their research. Erin knew what to look for. Guys who assaulted women as brutally as the killer had usually exhibited a pattern of escalation. Dahl would almost certainly have a history of violence. If he had an explosive temper, he'd probably have disorderly conduct busts.

She found nothing. His fingerprints weren't even in the system prior to this arrest. She wondered whether he'd moved from another jurisdiction, so she cast the net nationwide. An hour and a half later, she still had nothing.

"This guy's a ghost," she said. "Either he's a saint, or he's the cleverest, luckiest perp we've ever locked up."

"It could be his first major offense," Vic said. "Everyone's gotta start somewhere."

"There should be *something*," she insisted. "This guy doesn't have a parking ticket on his record. He's never been pulled over for speeding."

"He lives in downtown Manhattan," Vic said. "I don't think he owns a car."

"That's not the point. This is fishy."

"What, so now you think someone scrubbed his record?"

"That's a thought. But he doesn't seem like he's an organized-crime associate. Unless he's got serious pull with someone dirty in the department, it wouldn't happen."

"What do you know about him?" Vic asked, only too happy to leave his financial research to come over and see what Erin was doing.

"He's twenty-six, unmarried, living alone."

"In Yorkville? That's gonna be expensive."

"You turn up anything sketchy in his finances?"

"No," Vic sighed. "Everything looks normal so far."

"Looks like he grew up in the Bronx, won a scholarship to Columbia, graduated magna cum laude, got his Masters in History of Art and Design from the Pratt Institute two years ago. Then he did an internship at the Guggenheim and they hired him on completion. He's been there ever since."

"Not exactly a typical perp background," Vic said.

"I found an address for his mom," Erin said. "She still lives in the Bronx. I don't know about other family."

"Unmarried," Vic repeated. "What's his connection with the victim?"

"I don't know," she said. "I'm about to start her background. We'll see if anything matches up."

"Back to the spreadsheets for me," he said sadly.

It didn't take long for Erin to find the connection. "Got it!" she exclaimed.

"Got what?" Webb asked. He'd just gotten off the phone, still working on the mechanics of the upcoming lineup.

"I know how Dahl knows Bledsoe."

"Do tell," Webb said.

"She was in grad school, studying fine art."

"And she was hanging out at the Guggenheim a lot?" Vic guessed.

"Bingo."

"So she met the young, handsome exhibit prep guy," Webb said. "And romance blossomed into murder."

"Pretty much. How's the lineup coming, sir?"

"All set. Ryan Bledsoe's coming into the station in half an hour."

*   *   *

Lineups made for good police theater, but Erin didn't much like them in practice. There were all kinds of things that could go wrong. Eyewitness testimony was always unreliable, and that could be compounded by the weird environment of the lineup. The witness might be tipped off by one of the officers, either unintentionally or deliberately, to pick a particular subject. The suspect's lawyer needed to be present or the identification could be suppressed at trial. There was psychological pressure on the witness to pick someone from the lineup, whether they recognized the suspect or not. And, of course, if they picked the wrong guy, the whole exercise ended up damaging the case.

On the whole, Erin preferred fingerprints, or a confession, or a blood sample from the scene. But you had to take what the case had to give.

They were trying to do everything by the book. Curtis Dahl was lined up together with five other Black men of similar height and build, all either bald or with shaved heads; Erin knew two of them were Patrol officers who'd put on street clothes for the exercise. The other three were civilians. They were standing in a row under numbers, one through six. They'd specifically tried to find guys who looked alike, so the lawyer would have nothing to complain about.

Dahl's lawyer was standing in the gallery along with Erin, Vic, Webb, and Bledsoe. Erin had left Rolf upstairs. The lawyer wasn't a top-tier defense attorney, but he wasn't fresh out of law school doing pro bono work either. Dahl's job paid decently enough for him to afford reasonably good representation. This lawyer was a rising star named Bauman, young and energetic. He'd put up a hard fight if it went to court.

"Now, take your time," Webb said to Bledsoe. "Don't pick out a specific person unless you're sure. I want you to look at these six men. If one of them is the man you saw in your apartment lobby this morning, state which number he is. Do you understand?"

"Don't look at the police officers, please," Bauman said. "Just look through the window."

Bledsoe nodded. He turned to the glass and stared at the six men.

Erin held her breath and reminded herself not to give any reaction, not to look at Bledsoe or at any man in particular.

"That's him," Bledsoe said. "Number three."

"You're absolutely certain of that?" Webb asked.

"Absolutely."

Erin let out the breath. He'd picked out Dahl. No hesitation, no doubt. That was enough to charge him.

"Thank you," Webb said. "That will be all, Mr. Bledsoe. I apologize for calling you in again."

"My pleasure," he said. "Anything I can do to help. I want that bastard to pay for what he did to me."

"That's it," Webb said, after Bledsoe and Bauman had left the room and Patrol officers had returned Dahl to his holding cell. "That's our guy."

"Case closed?" Vic asked, half-seriously.

"Not even close," Webb retorted. "We haven't placed him in the room yet."

"But we've got him tied to the victim," Vic said. "And identified as being in the building, which is a direct contradiction of his statement."

"That's not enough for a conviction," Webb said.

"There's the wound on his hand, too," Erin said.

"That'll help," Webb said. "But it's still circumstantial. I'll tell Levine. We'll see if we can get any foreign skin samples from the victim. If we can match them to Dahl, that'll help."

"We doing anything in the meantime?" Vic asked.

"Just normal research."

"Wow," Erin said. "I get to clock out at a normal hour this evening. That's good. I've got a dinner with the family."

"Parents coming down?" Vic asked.

"No. Just my brother and his wife and kids, here in town."

"That's you," he said with a grin. "Always living on the edge. Try not to go too crazy."

*   *   *

Sean O'Reilly Junior, his wife Michelle, and their two children, Anna and Patrick, lived in a brownstone in Midtown Manhattan, a house Erin would never be able to afford on her police salary. Despite the difference in economic circumstances, Erin found her brother's life an odd but comforting throwback to her own childhood. Michelle was a smart, well-educated woman who had chosen to raise a family instead of pursue a career, enabled by Sean's high-paying medical position.

Immediately upon entering, Erin and Rolf were engulfed in Whirlwind Anna. Erin's nine-year-old niece flung her arms around her waist, then disengaged and grabbed Rolf. The big, tough police K-9 maintained what dignity he could, but allowed the young girl to manhandle him into the living room, where they commenced a game involving tunnels made from sofa cushions.

Sean was in the living room, calmly reading a newspaper while his daughter and Erin's dog weaved around him. He folded the paper and got up to give Erin a hug.

"Hey, kiddo," he said. "Twice in one day. I hope you left work at the office."

"Me, too," she said.

"Welcome," Michelle said from the kitchen doorway. She was a tall, attractive, dark-haired woman, French-Canadian by birth. Though an O'Reilly by marriage, she had adopted the entire clan as her own. She extended her arms to Erin, planting a kiss on her cheek.

"I'm not late for once," Erin said. "We wrapped things up on time today."

"Did you get the bad guy?" Michelle asked.

"Yeah. We grabbed him less than half a day after the crime. It's no departmental record, but it's a good day's work. Where's Patrick?"

"He's having a time-out."

"Uh oh," Erin said. "What's he doing time for?"

"When Sean came home from work, Anna climbed up on his lap. Patrick got jealous. We tell them to use their words, but he didn't want to use words. He bit Anna."

"Hmm," Erin said. "On the plus side, his juvenile record will be sealed when he turns eighteen, so it shouldn't affect his future employment prospects."

Michelle laughed. "I know, it's just one of life's little emergencies. I'll let him out of his room for dinner. I didn't know when you were coming, so I'll need a few minutes to get everything ready."

When they sat down to dinner, Anna was bright and cheerful, while Patrick sulked and acted the part of the victim.

Michelle proudly set her newest culinary concoction on the table.

"Okay, I give up," Erin said. "I haven't seen this before. What is it?"

"Duck confit with spicy pickled raisins," Michelle said.

"Eww! I don't want pickles!" Anna said, wrinkling her nose.

"Not pickles, dear, pickled raisins," her mother explained. "You can pickle almost any fruit or vegetable."

"Why would you want to?" Anna wondered.

Sean snorted a laugh, earning him a withering look from his wife.

"Should we say grace?" Erin said, smoothing over the moment. They obediently bowed their heads.

Erin liked the food, which surprised her. She knew Michelle was an excellent cook, but her own tastes ran toward simple home recipes, takeout, and pasta.

"This is fantastic, Shelley," she said, extending her plate for more.

"It doesn't taste like pickles," Anna added. One of her hands crept off the table.

"Don't feed Rolf from the table," Erin reminded her.

"I wasn't... much," her niece said sheepishly. A faint crunching and chewing was audible under the table.

"Rolf's not a pet, dear," Michelle said. "He's a working dog. He's Aunt Erin's partner."

"If Auntie Erin had a human partner, we'd feed him at the table," Anna argued.

"How did things go after you left the hospital?" Sean asked Erin.

"Oh! I didn't know you two ran into each other today," Michelle said. "Nothing too serious, I hope?"

"Shelley, I work Major Crimes," Erin said. "It's always something serious. We caught the guy."

"Already?" Sean asked.

"Yeah. Traced his phone off the victim's. Turns out it wasn't a random attack."

"Was it a murder?" Anna asked with morbid fascination.

"Yes." Erin didn't believe in lying to children.

"Of course you caught him," Anna said. "You always do."

"Not always," Erin said. "But we can usually figure out who did it."

"Score one for the good guys," Sean said.

"Yeah," Erin said. "At least he won't kill anyone else." But she said it thoughtfully. A part of her still wasn't completely convinced.

"You won't believe what Shelley's whipped up for dessert," Sean said.

"It's a berry galette," Michelle said. "With gourmet vanilla bean ice cream."

"I'm ready for dessert now," Anna announced, sliding her half-full plate away.

"That's not how this works, dear," Michelle said. "Three more bites. Big ones."

"Rolf can have what's left," Anna said.

"Raisins aren't good for dogs," Erin said.

"Then why are they good for people?"

"I'm a cop, kiddo, not a nutrition expert."

"Erin, can you help me dish up dessert out in the kitchen?" Michelle asked.

"Sure thing, sis." Erin stood and helped clear the table.

Once they were out in the kitchen, with a swinging door between them and the dining room, Michelle leaned in close to Erin. "So, how's it going?" she whispered conspiratorially.

"How's what going?" Erin asked, playing innocent.

"You know," Michelle said in an even lower tone. "Your gangster?"

"Shelley!" Erin hissed.

"I bet it's really romantic. All the cloak-and-dagger stuff, meeting at odd hours, the danger, the thrill."

"Shelley, danger isn't really romantic. Well, okay, I guess it can be, a little."

"Your mom's been after me. She knows I know something. She wants a name. How long are you going to keep this secret from your folks?"

"I was kind of hoping to keep them in the dark until an hour or two after my dad's funeral," Erin said, only half-joking. "See, he and my boyfriend know each other. From the old days. Professionally."

"Oh," Michelle said. Her eyes got wide. "Did Sean ever arrest him?"

"No, but they have a history."

"Wow. This is some Romeo and Juliet stuff," Michelle said.

"Remember what happened to Romeo and Juliet?" Erin countered.

"Well, yes, but you're smarter than Juliet. I believe in happy endings."

"The street doesn't have many of those. It's not Disneyland out there, Shelley."

Michelle sighed. "I know that, Erin. I'm a romantic, not an idiot." She leaned against the kitchen counter and looked at the ceiling. "I just don't want to believe this is all there is."

Erin looked at her sister-in-law. "What do you mean? You've got a great life. Two beautiful kids, this great house, a good husband... Well, okay, he's my big brother, so he's not all that, but the rest of it's still true."

"You want the truth, Erin? I'm a little jealous of you."

"Of me?" Erin repeated in astonishment.

"You've got this new, exciting thing going in your life," Michelle said. "I'm a dried-up old housewife. You know what's going to happen after you go home and I get the kids put down for the night?"

"Shelley, this is my brother we're talking about. I really don't need to know—"

"Nothing," Michelle said softly. "He'll go to sleep, because he's worn out from another long shift in the ER. But at least he's doing something with his life. I want adventures, Erin. I want to travel the world, see things, do things, meet people."

Erin was a little alarmed by this turn to the conversation. "Shelley, be careful," she said. "You've got a good thing going here. You don't want to screw it up."

"No," Michelle sighed. "But I just wish I could not be myself for a little while, for a week maybe, or a month."

"Sounds like you need a vacation," Erin said. "Talk to Sean about it. I bet you can make something happen."

"That's a good idea," Michelle said. "But I do want to meet this mystery man of yours sometime."

"One of these days," Erin said unconvincingly.

The berry galette was delicious, just the right mix of sweetness and tart fruit flavor. Erin left the brownstone with a pleasantly full stomach, but troubled by her conversation with her sister-in-law. Maybe the grass always was greener on the other side, she reflected. She'd often felt jealous of her brother's good fortune. Was she also jealous of Michelle's kids? That was a good question, and one she wasn't ready to answer right then.

But she did know she wanted to see her man again, even though she'd had lunch with him just a few hours before. That felt a very long time ago. She'd go home first, drop off Rolf, but then she was going to the Barley Corner. A good, strong drink with the man she loved would be the right way to finish up the day.

Chapter 6

The Barley Corner, on the surface, was a pleasant corner sports pub in Manhattan. But if you knew where to look, it had more criminals than a cell block in Riker's Island and more concealed weapons than a Secret Service detail. It was a money-laundering front and meeting spot for associates of the O'Malley branch of the Irish mob. But that was okay. The heavy hitters in the place all knew who Erin was and that, in addition to being a cop, she was Carlyle's girlfriend. She'd become a sort of unofficial mascot for the place. Word on the street was that she provided legal cover for the O'Malleys' daily operations, so she was a de facto wiseguy.

When Erin got there, she saw Carlyle at the bar. He was in the middle of a serious-looking conversation with a heavyset, tattooed Irishman. She recognized Caleb Carnahan, Carlyle's head security man. Ian Thompson was there, too, sitting by himself at a side table that offered a good view of the front door. Ian nodded politely to Erin, but looked away immediately. He was clearly on duty.

Caleb gave Erin a cold-eyed look as she walked up to the bar. She ignored him and spoke to Carlyle.

"Evening."

"Evening, darling." He stood up and motioned her to a seat. "Caleb and I were just finishing. If you'll excuse me just one moment longer."

"Sure." Erin raised a finger to Danny, the Corner's number-one bartender. Danny wasn't a mob guy; he actually was exactly what he appeared to be, a friendly young man with an uncanny memory for his customers and their favorite drinks.

"Usual, Erin?" Danny asked.

"Thanks."

A glass of Glen D whiskey accordingly appeared on the bar in front of her. She sipped it and tried to appear disinterested in Carlyle's conversation with his security chief.

"As I was saying, I'd like the lads to be particularly alert over the next few days, just on the off-chance," he said.

"You got it, boss," Caleb said. "You gonna be stayin' here, or goin' anywhere?"

"Just the usual routine, lad."

"You want anyone extra around the place?"

"I want two lads on hand at all hours, open or closed."

"You got it," Caleb repeated. "That all?"

"That's all for now. Good evening."

Caleb turned and lumbered back toward the small office under the stairs. It was the Corner's security station, a converted coat closet that housed the monitors for the pub's security cameras. Erin also suspected Carlyle kept it stocked with enough guns to refight the Irish War of Independence, ever since the Corner had been attacked the previous year. She'd never asked him to confirm this, and he hadn't offered any information on the subject.

"My apologies, darling," Carlyle said. "Just a bit of business."

"Expecting trouble?" she asked, cocking a head in the direction of Caleb's retreating back.

"Always."

"But you're taking extra precautions."

Carlyle nodded. He started to say something else, but was interrupted.

Erin was a street cop straight through to her backbone. She had very good instincts, but she was still caught completely off-guard. The newcomer was fast and came up on her blind side. Before she'd fully realized what was happening, a man had looped one arm around her waist and swept her off the barstool.

Her training and experience kicked in. She stomped at the man's instep with the heel of one foot, pivoted, and brought up her hand in an open-palm strike aimed to break his nose.

Her assailant was about her size and no stronger than she, but he was a hell of a lot faster. He nimbly slid his foot out from under her stomp, wrapping his leg around hers. His head weaved to the side and her hand hit nothing but air. Then he used his leg at her calf and his arm at her waist, gracefully turning their clinch into a sidelong dip, like a professional dancer would do to end a big musical number. Erin found herself stretched out diagonally, her lower back suspended by his arm, his knee bent just beneath her. She was looking straight into a pair of bright green eyes that sparkled with mischief and good humor.

"Corky," she growled.

Before she could go on, James Corcoran leaned in and planted a friendly kiss square on her startled lips. Then he spun her up and out again, leaving her standing a couple of feet away. He grinned.

"I've been wanting to do that for a good long while," he said.

"You do that again and you're likely to get shot," she said. "You shouldn't sneak up on a cop." But she couldn't help smiling. Corky was difficult to stay angry at, no matter how outrageous his behavior. He was the friendliest man in the Irish mob, on good terms with almost everyone, and was Carlyle's lifelong best friend. Though they'd grown up on the same street in Belfast, the two men could hardly be more different. Carlyle was all cool courtesy, control, and sharp-edged etiquette. Corky was as fiery as his bright red hair, impulsive, quick, trusting his luck. Erin had to admit Corky was lucky. It was the only reason she could think of why he hadn't been killed yet.

"That's my woman you're romancing, Corks," Carlyle said quietly. "Right in front of me. Is that how it's going to be?"

Corky laughed. "If she doesn't mind, why should you? Besides, if you're trusting her, you've nothing to fret over. She had her chance with me. I'm just giving her a wee taste of what she's been missing."

"I haven't seen you in a while," Erin said. "But that doesn't mean I've been missing you. How's things?"

"Oh, I'm grand," he said, seating himself on Erin's left and signaling Danny for a drink. "Double whiskey, there's a good lad. House brand."

"Not getting in too much trouble, I hope?" she said.

"Nothing I can't handle. I hope you're treating my mate right."

"You're not worried about how he's treating me?"

Corky picked up his whiskey and tossed off half of it at one gulp. He blinked as he swallowed. "Not Cars. He knows exactly how to treat a lady. Besides, you're more than capable of taking care of yourself. And how's your business?"

"Caught a murderer today."

"Grand! Anyone I know?"

"I doubt it." But Erin wasn't sure. Corky was one of those guys who seemed to know everyone.

"New case, or ongoing?" Carlyle asked.

"New one. Open and shut."

"Must have been a foolish killer," Corky said. "Or an unlucky one. Speaking of which, Cars, you hear about those lads in Belfast?"

"Those three UVF guys who were shot?" Erin asked.

Corky was startled. "You've a fine inside line on information yourself," he said, impressed. "Keeping your ear to the ground in the old country, are you?"

"Interpol," she explained.

"Ah," Corky said. "Those nosy gobshites don't know how to stay out of everyone's business."

"I just heard about that," Carlyle said. "I've taken steps."

"So that's what you were worried about?" Erin asked. "You had nothing to do with it. Did you?"

"That depends on one's perception of the situation," Carlyle said.

"How do you mean?"

"You're right, I'd no idea it was going down," he said. "But I'm not certain that's the appearance of it. And as I've told you before, appearance matters a great deal more than truth in such matters."

"You worried about the cops?" Erin asked.

Carlyle smiled and Corky laughed out loud. Both of them shook their heads.

"The Irish police haven't any jurisdiction on this side of the water," Carlyle explained. "And even if they had, they're the last lads I'd be concerned about."

"They couldn't find their own arses in a bright-lit room with the aid of both hands," Corky added.

"I'm more concerned with the UVF themselves," Carlyle went on. "They've been at rather loose ends since the Good Friday accords. They've a number of hardened killers on tap, and some of their people are right here in New York."

"You think they might come after you?" she asked. "In retaliation?"

"They think they know who did the shooting," Carlyle said. "Whether they're right or not, it's a person who's known to have a personal connection with me."

"And there's the other thing," Corky said.

Carlyle shot him a sharp look. "We needn't go into that."

Now Erin's curiosity was piqued. "What other thing?"

"It's nothing to be concerned about," Carlyle said.

Corky, either blind to Carlyle's deflection or, more likely, just not caring, went right ahead. "Bobby Coughlin, Bloody Bob they called him, was one of the lads who got it. And I'm only sad he got it quick. It's some consolation to think he's roasting in Hell as we're speaking. It's no more than he deserves."

"Bloody Bob Coughlin?" Erin repeated. "I never heard of him."

"You'd not know him," Carlyle said. "He never left Ireland. He was a killer for the UVF in the Nineties. He specialized in taking down folk in ambushes, usually in their own homes."

"He was a right bloody bastard," Corky said. "He'd kill a lad's whole family if he could."

"Was there a personal beef between you guys and this Bloody Bob?" Erin asked. Carlyle and Corky had both been with the IRA during that period. Carlyle had built bombs. She'd never been entirely sure what Corky had done; accounts conflicted.

"You might say that," Carlyle said. His lips had compressed to a thin line.

"We're of the opinion he was one of the lads who shot up my mate's flat," Corky said with uncharacteristic softness.

"Shot up your flat..." Erin said to Carlyle and trailed off as understanding hit her. The thing that had driven Carlyle to leave Ireland had been the murder of his wife. Rose McCann had been gunned down in their apartment while cooking dinner. She hadn't had anything to do with the IRA. She was just a country girl Carlyle had met, loved, and married, a sweet girl. Carlyle didn't like to talk about her, but he'd once confided to Erin that at the time of her murder, she'd been pregnant with what would have been their first child.

"Jesus Christ," she said.

"Sometimes it's a long time coming, but there's justice in this bloody world," Corky said in tones of bitter satisfaction. "Here's to the devil collecting his due." He drained the rest of his whiskey.

"Carlyle," Erin said. "Did Siobhan know? That Bloody Bill was a suspect?"

"I never told her," he said. "Why would I want to burden a lass with that sort of knowledge? Besides, you've met Siobhan. You know exactly what she'd have done, had she known."

"Yeah. Pretty much what she just did."

"Neither of us was there," he said. "We don't know for certain she pulled the trigger."

"But you think she did."

Carlyle nodded slowly. "It wouldn't surprise me."

"Does it make you happy?"

"Erin, I'll shed no tears for that bastard. But if killing Bob Coughlin would make me happy, he'd have been dead years ago. I've tried my hand at revenge and it's given me precious little satisfaction."

"I offered," Corky confided to Erin. "A few years back. He told me not to be a bloody fool."

"I'm a cop," Erin said. "Remember? You can't tell me those things."

"I've not forgotten," he said more cheerfully. "We're discussing a hypothetical act of revenge against a lad who's perfectly safe from me now. I'll wager where he is, there's nothing I could do that's worse than he's currently experiencing.

But now I'd best be off. I've some lads to speak with. The night's young."

"See you around, Corky," Erin said. "And seriously, don't grab me from behind again. Especially if Rolf's with me. He won't understand, and I don't care how fast you are, he'll rip your arm off and eat it."

"Promises," Corky said with a grin. Then he was gone.

Erin put a hand on Carlyle's arm. "Are you okay?" she asked quietly.

"Why wouldn't I be?"

She could feel the tension in his muscles through the sleeve of his coat. "I bet hearing about Coughlin brought back some... memories."

"Aye. That was something I thought I'd put behind me."

"Are you going to be all right?"

He nodded. "But I can't discount the possibility of retaliation, as I said. And these UVF lads, they're not like most men. They'll go for a lad's family, as Corky said. I was already thinking about this, and I think it's time we put it into effect. We need an emergency word."

"A what?"

"A word we can use, if either of us find ourselves in a situation with lads who mean us harm. It ought to be something commonplace, so they'll not be suspicious, but something we'd never normally say. That way, if you hear me say it, on the phone, or perhaps over a wiretap," he smiled wryly, "you'll know something's amiss."

"And I can come rescue you?"

"And you can stay the bloody hell away," he retorted. "I'll not have you getting killed on my behalf, Erin."

"If you're in danger, I'm coming to help," she shot back. "What did you have in mind?"

"I was thinking a term of endearment," he said.

"Like 'darling?'"

"Aye, but that's something I do say."

Erin thought about it. "How about 'sweetheart?' I've never called you that, and I know you've never said it to me."

"Grand. That'll be our secret, then. And I hope that's the last time I'll hear that word from your lips. Now don't you go forgetting and dropping it into everyday conversation."

"It's a deal," she said. "This conversation got a little dark. I think we need another drink."

"Now you're reading my thoughts," he said. "Danny! We'll be needing another round here."

Chapter 7

Erin got up early and drove Rolf to Central Park while it was still dark. Ian Thompson was already there. He nodded to her.

"Morning, ma'am."

"Morning."

With that, they started running. It had become their shared ritual, a quiet and calming start to the day. Being in Ian's company was almost like being alone. He didn't start conversations, didn't demand attention. Erin found his presence comforting. He was aware of everything, but in spite of his constant alertness, he had an inner stillness, probably a result of his sniper training. There was nobody Erin would rather have watching her back in a fight, not even Vic.

"How well do you know Caleb?" she asked as they jogged around the edge of The Pond in the southeast corner of the park.

"Know him a little, ma'am."

"Is he a friend of yours?"

"Supervisor."

"What's your take on him?"

"Why do you want to know, ma'am?"

"He doesn't seem to like me much."

Ian didn't seem overly concerned by this revelation. "You're a cop," he replied.

"And Caleb's in the Life," Erin said. "Does he think I'm a bad influence?"

"He thinks you're an influence," Ian said. "He giving you trouble?"

"No. He hardly talks to me."

"You want him to?"

"I don't know. Not really, I guess."

"Then what's the problem, ma'am?"

"Does Carlyle trust him?"

"He handles Mr. Carlyle's security," Ian said as if that answered the question. Erin supposed it did. Carlyle had survived several attempts on his life. He was far too smart not to have bodyguards he trusted.

"I guess I'd feel better if it was you," Erin said.

"What do you mean, ma'am?"

"Running security at the Corner."

"I'm no officer, ma'am. I like what I'm doing."

His tone put an end to that conversation. But Erin kept thinking about it as they ran. She'd met plenty of wiseguys, including some who made her much more uncomfortable than Caleb Carnahan. Mickey Connor and Evan O'Malley, for instance. Still, something about Caleb rubbed her a little wrong. She decided to look him up when she got to work, just to be thorough. She ought to know Carlyle's close associates.

They finished their jog and parted company. Erin took Rolf home, showered, and grabbed a quick breakfast. Then it was back to the precinct and the grind of Major Crimes.

Webb was in the office when she arrived. "Lawyers," was the first word out of his mouth when he saw her.

"What about them?" she answered. "I hate them too."

"That weasel Bauman," Webb said, "must have been up all night prepping his paperwork. He's filed complaints with the DA's office and at One PP with the Commissioner."

"Complaints? What the hell for?"

"Racial profiling, for starters. He's alleging we had insufficient evidence to charge his client and he's requesting Dahl be ROR." Webb meant the lawyer was asking Dahl be released on his own recognizance, without bail.

"He does know this is a murder case, right?" Erin said. "Depending on the judge, he might not even get bail."

"He's holding a press conference later today," Webb went on. "He's engaging the NAACP and the ACLU and everyone else he can think of. He's doing an online fundraiser to hire more lawyers."

"That's got nothing to do with us," Erin said. "We've got a good case."

"We'd better," Webb said darkly. "Because this case is going to get political. It'll have a spotlight shining right on it. CSU sent over a bunch of stuff late last night. Neshenko's down in Evidence getting it logged. Go down there with him and see what we've got. I want hard physical evidence tying our guy to the scene. One eyewitness who saw him in the building isn't good enough. We need to place him in that room."

Erin accordingly went to the evidence locker. Rolf stuck by her side. He didn't get to go into the evidence room often, and it was full of interesting smells. His nose twitched eagerly and his ears were perked to full upright position.

She found Vic talking to the officer in charge of the evidence room. He had several boxes of stuff on the counter. Vic looked both awake and pleased, which wasn't typical for this hour of morning. Erin credited his sort-of-girlfriend, a Street Narcotics cop who worked nights. Zofia Piekarski was an energetic street cop who, according to Vic, tended to be pretty keyed up when she got off duty around five in the morning.

"Hey, Vic," Erin said. "Webb sent me to see what we've got."

"We've got our guy's prints at the scene," Vic said triumphantly.

"You're sure?"

"Just checked them against Dahl. He was there all right."

"Where'd you find the prints?"

"Doorknob, living room, bathroom. Hell, he was all over the place."

"Hammer?"

"No, the hammer was wiped clean."

"That seem a little weird to you? That he'd leave his prints everywhere, but would be careful to clean off the tool he used to make entry?"

"Erin, what do you want? Webb asked for something tying him to the scene, and we've tied him to the scene. We got a witness putting him in the lobby. We got messages from him on the victim's phone. You want me to gift-wrap the son of a bitch for you? Are you trying to piss me off? Because it won't work. This is gonna be a good day for me."

Erin raised her hands in mock surrender. "Okay, okay. Any other prints?"

"Of course. Two sets. One belonging to our victim, the others from her husband. We got elimination prints from him yesterday when he came in for the lineup."

"That's it?"

"That's it."

"I guess they didn't have many visitors."

Vic shrugged. "Makes our job easier."

"Webb says Dahl's lawyer is making a stink downtown."

"He can make all the stink he wants. He's the one who'll end up smelling bad. I'm telling you, Erin, we've got his guy dead to rights. I bet if we take another run at him, he'll crack."

"Let's try it," Erin said. "If we get a confession, it'll be the bow on top of the package."

* * *

With Webb's approval, Erin and Vic sat down in the interrogation room with Dahl and Bauman. Vic would be playing the "bad cop" role this time. Dahl looked pretty lousy. He was unshaven and hollow-eyed. Erin thought maybe he'd been crying.

Bauman, on the other hand, was sharply dressed, bright-eyed, and ready for trouble. He watched the detectives carefully, a professional ready to do good work.

"You wanna change your story?" Vic said.

"My client has nothing to add at this time," Bauman said.

"So you weren't in the Hope Building yesterday?" Vic went on.

"That's right," Dahl said.

Bauman glanced at Dahl, who made a gesture with his hand, indicating he was all right.

"So you'd be surprised to learn we've got your fingerprints all over the Bledsoe apartment?" Vic asked.

Dahl flinched, but he met Vic's eyes directly. "I never said I wasn't in the apartment," he said quietly.

"Do not say another word," Bauman said, tight-lipped.

"You said it fifteen seconds ago," Vic retorted.

"I said I wasn't there yesterday," Dahl said, ignoring his lawyer.

"Mr. Dahl," Bauman said warningly.

"Yes, I've been there," Dahl said. "On other days."

"So you knew Amelia Bledsoe," Vic said.

"You know I did."

Bauman looked at the ceiling, as if hoping to find an easier client there. "Mr. Dahl was not at the scene of the crime when the crime occurred," he said. "That's the only relevant detail."

"You were putting it to Amelia, weren't you," Vic said with deliberate crudeness. "While her husband was out."

"Detective, that's completely inappropriate and unwarranted," Bauman said. "It also plays on sexual and racial stereotypes."

"And it's not true," Dahl said.

"You claim you weren't physically involved with Amelia Bledsoe?" Vic asked.

"Again, this is irrelevant to my client's situation," Bauman said.

"Curtis," Erin said softly. "What was the nature of your relationship with Amelia?"

"She was my friend."

"That's it?" Vic said in disbelief. "You expect us to believe that?"

"I don't expect you to believe me at all," Dahl said, enunciating each word very precisely. "You got me, you've convinced yourself I did this, so of course you'll assume I'm lying, whatever I say."

"Mr. Dahl, please stop talking now," Bauman said.

"Convince us," Vic said.

"Amelia is... was a wonderful woman," Dahl said. "I met her at the museum. She was studying James Turrell's project in the rotunda."

"When was this?" Erin interjected.

"Last August. The centerpiece of the exhibition was a reimagining of the rotunda into a Skyspace. The work was called *Aten Reign*."

"Want to repeat that?" Vic said. "In English?"

"It was a light show, basically," Dahl said. "It's hard to describe if you haven't seen it. It used the space itself as an integral part of the exhibition. I walked Mr. Turrell through the space and helped with some minor aspects of the presentation. It was impressive. Amelia was taking a course on the use of light in modern art, so of course she came to the exhibition on several occasions."

"And you just happened to start talking to her?" Vic asked.

"She asked me some questions and we started talking. We had a number of interests in common. She kept coming back to the museum, and over the next few months, we became friends."

"Did she give you the impression she was interested in you?" Erin asked. "Maybe as more than friends?"

"At first I thought maybe she was," Dahl said.

"Mr. Dahl—" Bauman began warningly.

"And that was pretty awkward," Dahl said.

"Because she was married?" Vic asked.

"Because I wasn't interested in her. Not that way."

"She was a pretty young woman," Vic said.

"Exactly," Dahl said.

Vic blinked. "Oh."

"You're saying you're gay?" Erin asked Dahl.

He nodded.

"You didn't say anything about this before," she said.

"Would being a member of two different minorities help my situation?" he retorted. "It's not something I advertise to strangers."

"Did Amelia know about your orientation?" Erin asked.

"Yes. I told her back in January. I didn't want any misunderstandings."

"How did she react?"

"I think she was a little disappointed," Dahl said. "But she said she felt safe around me."

Vic snorted.

"Detective, please," Bauman said.

"Allergies," Vic said, unconvincingly.

Erin was thinking about what Dahl had just said. "Did Amelia feel unsafe elsewhere?" she asked.

"Yes."

"Where?"

"At home."

Erin hadn't been expecting that. "What do you mean?" she asked.

"Amelia didn't feel safe at home. With her husband."

"Why not?" Erin asked.

"She felt like he was always trying to control her," he said. "He made her leave her phone unlocked so he could check her message history. He checked her Internet browsing. He kept asking questions about where she was, who she was with, that sort of thing. It was making her nervous."

"Why did you go to their apartment?" Erin asked.

"She was having panic attacks. I was afraid maybe she might be having a nervous breakdown, that she might hurt herself. She'd call me sometimes, when she felt anxious, and I would go and sit with her and talk with her."

"And that's all you did?" Vic asked.

"Sometimes I'd hold her."

"How sweet," Vic said.

Bauman stood up abruptly. "This interview is over," he said.

"Would that have anything to do with not wanting to be late for your press conference?" Vic asked.

"Just one more question," Erin said. "Curtis, was Amelia ever injured? Did anyone ever hurt her?"

Dahl hesitated. "I'm not sure," he said. "I thought maybe, and I asked her once, but she didn't answer."

"For the last time, Mr. Dahl, you're under no obligation to talk to them," Bauman said. "I'm going to continue working for you. And these detectives can think about how long they want to keep an innocent man locked up. I'm sorry I can't get you released yet, but I will, and the longer it takes, the worse they're going to look. I know some excellent people if you want to file a lawsuit against the city."

"And I'm sure you're not trying to intimidate the City of New York with the threat of a lawsuit," Vic said in a voice dripping with insincere sweetness.

That was the note on which the interview ended. Dahl went back to his cell, Bauman left the precinct to go to City Hall and face the news cameras, and Vic and Erin went back upstairs to Major Crimes.

"I think he's full of shit," was Vic's verdict.

"I don't know about that," Erin said.

"What, you buy that whole gay best friend song-and-dance?" Vic demanded. "He'd say anything to get out of trouble."

"Yeah," Erin said, but she wasn't sure. Dahl had planted some doubts in her mind. And if he'd been able to do that to her, his lawyer could definitely supply reasonable doubt to a jury. Their case wasn't airtight. When they got back to the office, Erin went to her phone and dialed the morgue.

"Levine, Morgue," the Medical Examiner said.

"Sometimes I think you live there, Doc," Erin said. "Can you check something on the Bledsoe case?"

"Yes."

"I want you to look for old injuries, partially-healed bruises, remodeled bones, that sort of thing. I'm looking for signs of systematic abuse."

"I'll look. Mr. Bledsoe has requested the body be released."

"Don't release it," Erin said sharply. "We need to hold onto it until we're sure what happened."

"I'll keep it," Levine said. "I'll send you my report as soon as I've completed it." She hung up without waiting for Erin's response.

Vic was watching Erin. "What, so now you think the husband was beating her?"

"I'm just trying to figure out what happened."

"You're doing the defense team's job for them," he said.

"We're trying to find the truth, Vic. The defense attorney isn't our enemy."

"Says you," Vic said. "You know how many stone-cold guilty perps walk because of guys like Bauman?"

"If they walk, it's because we didn't do our job right," Erin countered.

"Sometimes, Erin, I don't understand you. You've been a cop for what, twelve years? And you've still got this idealistic streak in you. I think you're nuts. It's all lawyers and juries. Those are the people we've got to worry about."

"Vic, juries are made of citizens."

"Civilians, you mean."

"We can't all be cops."

"Admit it, our job would be easier if we were." He grinned. "Okay, do your research. I'm still having a good day, and you can't stop me."

Chapter 8

Erin had two people to look up, one pertaining to the case, the other personal. She decided to hit Caleb Carnahan first and get him out of the way. The NYPD had a significant file on him. He was a career mobster who'd gotten his start in Brooklyn back in the early '90s. He'd been associated with Evan O'Malley for a very long time; longer even than Carlyle. Caleb was older than he looked. He was forty-two years old, eight of which he'd spent in prison for attempted murder. The victim had been an associate of the Lucarelli Mafia family, and while the Italian had survived, he'd been permanently crippled due to a bullet in the spine.

Caleb looked like old-school Mob muscle, a solid, reliable thug who'd do anything his boss told him to. Erin was a little surprised Carlyle was using him. She knew Carlyle valued personal relationships and direct loyalty above all else, and she would have expected him to have one of his own people as his head of security. She made a mental note to ask him about Caleb the next time they were alone.

Then it was Ryan Bledsoe's turn. What she found was a restraining order from an old girlfriend and a battery complaint, five years old. The complaint hadn't resulted in a trial. The young woman had retracted it, an all-too-common occurrence in Erin's experience. She also found several disorderly conduct misdemeanors from Bledsoe's teenage years. He'd gotten in fights, apparently, back in high school.

None of that was out of the ordinary. Lots of kids got in fights. Erin had thrown a few punches in school herself. But a restraining order was unusual enough to get her attention. She looked up the relevant information and found the girl, Carmen Sanchez. According to the police database, Sanchez still lived and worked in New York, with an address in SoHo. Her workplace was listed as a coffee shop called, appropriately enough, About Coffee.

She called the shop. A woman answered.

"About Coffee, how can I help you?"

"Hello. My name's Erin O'Reilly. I'm with the NYPD. Do you have a Carmen Sanchez working there?"

"Yeah, she's on the counter. Is everything okay?"

"Yes, she's not in any trouble. I'd just like to speak with her about someone she knows. Will she be there for the next hour or so?"

"Yeah, she's on until four."

"Okay, thanks."

Erin hung up and stood up from her desk. Rolf immediately bounced to his feet, hoping to get out of the office.

Webb gave her a look. "Going somewhere, O'Reilly?"

"Yes, sir. I've got a line on one of Ryan Bledsoe's exes. I want to talk to her."

"About what?"

"What he was like as a boyfriend."

"Why?"

"Because I want to know how far we can trust Bledsoe's testimony."

Webb raised an eyebrow. "So now you think the husband's lying?"

"I don't know what to believe right now. But Dahl doesn't feel right for this."

"O'Reilly, we know he was in the apartment. He's our best suspect. Come to that, he's our only suspect."

"Just let me look at this, sir."

Webb shrugged. "I'm not the one paying your salary. But we'll need more than a hunch if you're going to run this case off the rails."

Erin nodded. "*Komm,*" she told Rolf, twitching the leash.

Rolf thought Erin's idea was a great one. He was one hundred percent on board.

*   *   *

About Coffee was a narrow shop of whitewashed brick in west SoHo. It was an artsy, tree-lined neighborhood Erin didn't know very well. She saw numerous bicycles parked out front. It appeared to be a cozy little local hangout, off the beaten path. She led Rolf in the front door.

"Excuse me, ma'am," said the pretty, black-haired woman behind the counter. "I'm sorry, but no pets inside. Orders of the Health Department."

"He's a police K-9," Erin said, showing her shield.

The woman smiled. "That's okay, then. It's nothing personal, you understand. I love dogs." She gave Rolf a warm look. He returned it with his usual cool reserve.

"So, what can I get you, Officer?" the woman asked. "I don't think I've seen you around here. Are you new on this beat? Officer Nordheim comes in sometimes. Do you know him?"

Erin laughed. "One question at a time, ma'am. My name's Erin O'Reilly. I'm not walking a beat. I'm with Major Crimes, so I'm afraid I don't know Nordheim. I'm a detective."

"Oh! I didn't know detectives used dogs."

"Most of us don't. Rolf's a special case." Erin smiled down at her partner.

"That's great," the woman said. "So, what can I get you? Our coffee beans are roasted right here. I recommend the Caffe Cardamo. Just four-fifty, and it's amazing. You'll never want to go back to Starbucks after you try it."

"I'm not actually here for the coffee," Erin said. "I'm looking for Carmen Sanchez. Would that be you?"

"Yes." The woman looked confused. "But I don't understand why a detective would... Oh no, it's not my mom, is it?"

"No," Erin said. "I don't know anything about your mother. Is she in trouble?"

"Oh, thank God," Sanchez said. "She had a mild heart attack last week, and they just sent her home. I thought maybe... never mind. I'm sorry. People say I talk too much."

"I was hoping to talk to you about someone you know," Erin said. She looked around. The shop was very small and mostly full of people, some of whom were watching her curiously. "Can someone cover the counter for you for a few minutes?"

"I guess so." Sanchez turned and called over her shoulder, "Roz! Can you come up front for a minute?"

Roz agreed to mind the shop, and Erin accordingly stepped outside with Sanchez. They stood against a metal railing a short distance from the front door. Rolf sniffed Sanchez with interest. He'd never met someone who smelled so much like coffee.

"This is about Ryan Bledsoe," Erin said, watching the other woman's face for a reaction.

"Ryan?" Sanchez said. Her open, friendly face suddenly became wary. "Look, I don't want to get anyone in trouble. I know I shouldn't have filed that stupid report. It was nothing but headaches, start to finish."

"Why did you file the restraining order?"

"I overreacted. I mean, it's not like I was actually in danger or anything. We're not talking *Fatal Attraction* or whatever."

Erin nodded. "Go on, please."

"I just got a little spooked is all," Sanchez said. "Ryan and I had this fight and I broke up with him. He got kind of crazy."

"Crazy how?"

"He was all suspicious, always wanted to know what I was doing, who I was seeing. He thought I had another boyfriend."

"Did you?"

"No. But it wasn't any of his business, and I finally told him so. He grabbed me and tossed me down, and I thought he was going to hit me. He had this look in his eyes, I haven't ever seen anyone look at me that way."

"What did he do?" Erin asked softly.

Sanchez shrugged. "We were at a party. It was in college, you know? We were a little drunk, and so was everyone else. There was this other couple, they kind of fell through the door right then. I think they were looking for a place to hook up. They giggled and apologized, and Ryan got off me and I got out of there."

"But you filed a complaint?"

"Yeah. I told my roommate what had happened, and she said something about the conspiracy of silence and that if I didn't say something, he'd hurt someone else. And then it would be my fault too, because I could have stopped him. The way she was acting, it was like she thought he was going to stick me in a wood chipper or something." Sanchez rolled her eyes. "So I went to the campus police, and they completely blew me off, and then I went to the real cops. So it was this huge mess, and the Dean got involved, and they called my parents, and the way they were treating it, I started feeling like the bad guy. So I dropped the whole thing."

Erin nodded. "It's hard reporting that sort of situation," she said. "Were you genuinely frightened of Ryan? Or were you going completely on your roommate's advice?"

Sanchez shifted uncomfortably. "I don't know. I mean, yeah, for a second there, I thought he was going to beat me up or something. The way he grabbed me... but then, afterward, I thought it wasn't such a big deal. Hey, what are the police asking about Ryan for, anyway? You wouldn't be asking if something else hadn't happened. I mean, that was years ago. And you said you were with Major Crimes. That's, like, bank robberies and murders and stuff, right?"

"That's right," Erin said quietly.

"So what's that got to do with me?"

"I can't disclose information on a current investigation," Erin said, thinking this cheerful young woman really didn't want to know what had happened.

"Oh. I guess not. So, what else do you want to know?"

"I think that's everything I need for now," Erin said. She handed Sanchez one of her cards. "In case you think of anything we ought to know, you can call me at this number."

"I don't think I know anything about robberies and murders," Sanchez said. "But okay. You sure you don't want a cup of coffee? It's really, really good."

Erin started to refuse, then hesitated. "Sure, why not? I'll try that... what did you call it?"

"Caffe Cardamo. It's one of our specialties. You'll love it."

"How do you know that, ma'am?"

Sanchez gave her a brilliant smile. "Because everyone does."

*   *   *

Erin left the coffee shop with an excellent cup of Caffe Cardamo and a bunch of new questions. She called Webb from her car.

"How did your hunch play out?" he asked.

"We've got a problem, sir," she said.

"Is this a one-cigarette problem?"

"You tell me, sir. I don't smoke. Bledsoe has a history of violence. Against women."

"And Dahl doesn't." Webb sighed heavily. "This calls for a whole pack."

"I talked to the woman who filed the restraining order on Bledsoe," she went on. "She says he was controlling, unpleasant, always wanting access to her personal communications."

"That explains why Amelia's phone wasn't secured," Webb said. "So, what do you think? You think Bledsoe killed his wife?"

"I don't know. I like him better for it than Dahl."

"But it still could be either," Webb said. "Or none of the above. An intruder wearing gloves wouldn't have left prints anywhere, which would explain the clean hammer. Maybe Bledsoe is telling the truth about seeing a suspicious guy in the lobby."

"He identified Dahl in the lineup," Erin reminded him.

"That's true, but suppose he remembered him from a previous meeting?" Webb countered. "Then he saw a guy who looked kind of like this guy. Remember his description of the suspect's clothing? It didn't match what Dahl was wearing at the Guggenheim later that day."

"That's true," Erin said. "So you think he screwed up the ID at the lineup?"

"It's possible," Webb said. "A lot of people have trouble remembering faces outside their own ethnic group. Cops aren't the only people who profile."

"So what do we do, sir?"

"Bauman just finished his press conference," Webb said dryly. "He was all over the network news. We can't very well put out a BOLO now for bald-headed Black men. Can you imagine what the Commissioner would say?"

Erin could. None of it would be good. "We can't trust the eyewitness testimony anyway," she said. "We shouldn't have put so much weight on it in the first place."

"It matched with Dahl's description," Webb reminded her. "And the phone number was a match. It was a good arrest."

"I'm not sure about that," Erin said.

"It's a little late to be getting buyer's remorse, O'Reilly."

"Yes, sir. I know. What's our next step?"

"We're going to release Dahl. Without bail. I'm doing it now, before the Commissioner has the chance to order us to do it. That'll save Captain Holliday some heartburn. So much for an easy close."

"We need evidence," Erin said.

"You're starting to sound like me," Webb said. "Come back to the Eightball and regroup."

"On my way." Erin hung up and started the car.

*   *   *

Dahl was already gone by the time she got back to the precinct. Vic and Webb were in the Major Crimes office. Vic no longer looked like he was having a good day.

"Goddamned mess," was his opinion. "This one was supposed to be simple."

"We couldn't hold him," Erin said. "Not with what we had."

"It looks like we caved in to publicity and political pressure," he growled.

"There's no shame in that," Webb said. "It's a fine New York tradition."

"What would you know about that, sir?" Vic shot back. "You're from LA."

"We've got politics there, too. And racial politics, which are the messiest kind. It's even crazier there than here."

"Did we get anything from Levine yet?" Erin asked.

"Yeah," Vic said. "The report should be on your computer."

Erin checked it. Levine laid it out in clinical detail. Amelia Bledsoe had signs of several partially-healed minor injuries. The Medical Examiner had found bone remodeling indicative of a healed hairline fracture of the cheekbone and clavicle. She'd also discovered several partly-healed bruises. Any one of them by itself wouldn't be a big deal, but together, they told a story.

"Amelia was being abused," she announced. "Looks like whoever hit her did it hard enough to break her cheekbone once, and she had a fractured collarbone."

"The collarbone could be anything," Vic said. "Hell, I've broken both of mine. Twice each."

"And she had old bruises on her face and upper body," Erin added.

"Okay," Vic said. "So her asshole husband was hitting her."

"Someone was," Webb said. "Or at least someone did once. How old are the injuries?"

Erin consulted the report. "According to Levine, the broken bones are at least a month old. The bruises are more like four or five days."

"Not just one incident, then," Webb said. "Okay, I'm convinced."

The three detectives nodded to one another. All of them knew that systematic abuse was almost always perpetrated by a spouse, lover, or family member.

"Okay," Vic said again, standing up. "I'll go get the husband."

"Sit down, Neshenko," Webb said. "We jumped the gun once already. What are you going to charge him with?"

"Personally, I'm just hoping he resists arrest," Vic said, cracking his knuckles. He didn't like men who hurt women.

"I said, sit down," Webb said coldly.

Vic sat, sulkily.

"The old injuries are useless unless we can make a case for the murder," Webb said. "What do we have? Fingerprints? Tissue samples? The guy lives there. None of those are conclusive."

"Did you hear the way he talked, when he was here?" Erin asked.

"What about it?" Vic asked.

"Everything was about himself. It was all 'me, me, me,'" she said. "How many times did he even say Amelia's name?"

"You're right," Vic said, nodding. "He talked about her like she was something he owned. How come I didn't pick up on that?"

"You're a man," Erin said.

Vic bristled. "Hold on there. Don't you dare put me in a box with that jerk. I have never hit a woman in my life. And I've hit plenty of guys."

"That wasn't what I meant," she said. "I just meant, women are more likely to notice the way men talk about them." She paused. "You saying you wouldn't hit me if the situation called for it?"

Vic blinked. Then he laughed. "No, I'd make an exception for you. Wanna step outside right now?"

"How about, instead of committing misdemeanors on each other, we focus on the case?" Webb suggested. "As I see it, we have three theories right now. One, Curtis Dahl was in an affair with Amelia Bledsoe. She broke it off, he snapped and killed her in a rage. Two, Ryan Bledsoe believed Amelia was having an affair, he snapped and killed her in a rage. Three, an unknown intruder broke into the Bledsoe apartment and killed Amelia in the course of a botched robbery."

"Was he in a rage, too?" Vic inquired.

Webb gave him a weary look. "What possible difference does that make?"

"Just wondering."

"That's a good thing for you to be wondering, because you're on theory number three," Webb told him. "I want you to check other home invasion robberies in the area. See if any of them fit this MO, particularly if any also included assaults. If you get any possible matches, see if we've got any descriptions of possible intruders. I'll keep working the Dahl angle. Just because Bledsoe's lost some credibility doesn't mean he might not be telling the truth. O'Reilly, you're on Bledsoe. This was your idea, so you get to carry it."

Erin and Vic nodded. Vic settled himself behind his desk, muttering about how many robberies happened every year in Manhattan. Erin knew he just liked to bitch. He'd get the job done, and he'd do it well.

She had to think about how to approach her appointed part of the case. She couldn't ask Amelia about Ryan's behavior, but victims' words could sometimes be dragged out of the past. The first thing she did was call the precinct forensic techs and ask them to retrieve everything they could from Amelia's phone. Maybe there'd be something incriminating, or at least enlightening, in her deleted messages.

While they set to work on that project, she started calling grad-school art departments, wishing she'd asked Dahl which school Amelia had been attending. She made a guess and tried the Pratt Institute in Brooklyn first, reasoning that if Dahl had gotten his internship at the Guggenheim through them, Amelia might be enrolled in the same school.

Intuition, or luck, was with her. Amelia Bledsoe had been enrolled there, in the second year of a graduate program in Arts and Cultural Management. That program was located in the Manhattan satellite branch of the Institute, up on West 14th Street. Erin accordingly loaded Rolf into the Charger again and set off.

She tried to plan while she worked her way through the Manhattan traffic. She needed information on Amelia's friends and associates. So far, the only person Amelia had confided in was Dahl, and they couldn't completely trust his testimony.

Erin parked in the police space near the Institute and went in. After a couple of wrong turns, she ended up at the office of the Arts and Cultural Management chair. The name Delacroix was on the door.

"Come in," he said in answer to her knock. She opened the door and saw a spacious corner office adorned with promotional materials and memorabilia from museums around the world. Seated behind a very modern-style desk was a gray-haired man wearing a black leather jacket with silver chains. He looked to Erin like an aging motorcycle enthusiast who'd managed to stay thin.

"Professor Delacroix?" Erin asked.

"In the flesh." He stood up and extended a hand. "And you would be...?"

"Detective O'Reilly, NYPD," she said, taking the offered hand. She saw a tattoo on the back of his hand. It looked like that famous Norwegian painting, *The Scream*. "And this is Rolf, my K-9."

Rolf studied the man with a professional eye.

Delacroix raised an eyebrow. "Detective? Well, that's unexpected. Whatever you've got to say, I hope it can be kept short. I have a lecture in fifteen minutes."

"I'll be quick. I'm here about Amelia Bledsoe. Does that name ring a bell?"

"Amelia," Delacroix said thoughtfully. "She'd be, hmm, a brunette, pleasant face, interested in museum lighting and presentation?"

"That's her," Erin said. "How well do you know her?"

"Not well, I'm afraid," he said. "We have a sizable program, and I can't get to know all of the students as well as I'd like."

"Do you know if she had any close friends in the program?"

Delacroix shook his head. "No. Now that I think of it, she's a very quiet, withdrawn young woman. Rarely speaks up in class. But she pays attention. Good memory, good grades. Keen eye for light. She might do well in photography."

"How about teachers? Would you say she'd developed a good relationship with any of the faculty?"

"I'm sorry, Detective. I really can't think of anyone. I have the impression she wants to keep in the background. You know how it is. Every class has its eager participants, its slackers, and the ones who sit at the back and just soak everything in. Amelia is an excellent student, but not an outgoing one."

"Thanks." Erin swallowed her disappointment. "Your institution is connected with the Guggenheim. Do you know anything about that museum?"

Delacroix smiled. "More than I could possibly tell you in the twelve minutes we now have available. I bring my classes there on a frequent basis."

"Did you ever notice anything suspicious about anyone at the museum? Any of the staff, particularly?"

"Detective, when you go to a museum, do you look at the people who work there, or do you look at the art?"

"Both, Professor," Erin said dryly.

Delacroix paused and looked more closely at her face. "What did you say your name was, Detective?"

"O'Reilly."

He snapped his fingers. "Of course! I remember now! Last year, that lost Raphael painting which was stolen from the Queens Museum! I should have placed you from your dog. I read all about that incident in the *Times*. That story made quite a stir in the art community. The Renaissance masters aren't really my thing, of course. I tend toward more modern artists. But still, congratulations on your excellent work."

"Thank you. I just have one more question. Can you think of anyone who might have wanted to hurt Amelia?"

"No one at all," he said. "A sweet, harmless girl with a soul made of light. Excuse me, but is there something I ought to know about Amelia?"

"I'm sure it'll be in the *Times*," Erin said. "Thank you for speaking with me, Professor."

Chapter 9

Erin decided to grab a burger at the Corner on the way back to the precinct. Maybe the food would help her think through her next step. The police space near the pub was occupied by an NYPD patrol car, so she parked down the block.

As she unloaded Rolf from the Charger, her eye was caught by a familiar shock of curly red hair among the pedestrians. She walked quickly up behind the guy and took a moment to make sure of her identification. It was Corky, no doubt about it. He wouldn't be sneaking up on her this time.

"James Corcoran," she growled. "You're under arrest."

He spun around, moving with his trademark uncanny speed. She was pleased to note he held his hands up and out, not reaching into his pocket for a weapon. If he ever did get arrested, he'd do well to keep those hands in plain view. Then he saw her and a wide grin stretched across his face.

"Fair play, love," he said. "You got me right and proper. I suppose I may have deserved—"

The smile froze on his face. He was looking past Erin, into the street. "Down!" he snapped. Then he dove for the pavement behind a parked sedan.

Erin reacted almost as fast. Before she'd taken the time to think things through, she was dropping into a crouch, pulling her sidearm and turning in the direction Corky had been looking. She saw a black Chevy Tahoe, the back window on the side nearest her rolled down, the unmistakable muzzle of a rifle poking out.

"Everybody down!" Erin shouted. "Gun!" She didn't have a clean shot. She was surrounded by civilians, with more on the far side of the street. Somebody screamed. Then the rifleman started firing.

The reports of the gunshots echoed off the buildings on either side of the street, hard percussions hammering into her eardrums. More people screamed. Erin knelt behind the engine block of the car Corky was hiding behind. She felt the car tremble as high-caliber bullets punched through the bodywork. Three holes blasted out the passenger door between her and Corky, leaving jagged exit wounds like the petals of weird metal flowers. Rolf was right beside her, stiff-legged and bristling.

Erin swallowed her fear and came up, Glock in hand, resting the gun on the hood of the car. She took quick aim and fired twice at the Tahoe's window. She saw one bullet hit the door panel, stripping off the paint in a silver starburst. The other shot went into the vehicle, but she didn't know if she'd hit anyone. Then, with a squeal of rubber, the car sped away, taking the turn fast, narrowly missing the cross traffic.

A pair of Patrol officers rushed out of a nearby building, guns in hand. Erin whipped out her shield and held it up.

"At least one shooter, plus the driver," she said. "Black Chevy Tahoe, bullet hole in the left rear door. Didn't get the plate. I think the first number was a five."

"Copy," one of the officers said, sprinting toward their squad car. The other stood beside Erin, looking around. People lay everywhere, sprawled on the concrete. Erin looked for telltale bloodstains and didn't see any.

"Anyone hurt?" she called. "Anyone?"

Several people cautiously got to their feet. It didn't look like a single bullet had made contact with human flesh. That didn't surprise Erin much. Amateurs tended to assume just spraying a lot of lead around would guarantee a hit, but she'd been in enough gunfights to know that most bullets missed. In a drive-by shooting like this one, firing from an unstable, moving platform, the shooter would have had to be either a professional or lucky to hit his intended target.

"That was exciting, love," Corky said. He was up again, still smiling, not looking even the least bit alarmed. "Shall we have ourselves a wee nip, to calm our nerves?"

"Not right now," she said. She holstered her sidearm and walked out into the street, checking the other side of the car that had provided their cover. The streetward side was pockmarked with bullet holes. Her training, which had taught her the engine block offered the best protection, had been vindicated. Several bullets had been foiled by the big chunk of Detroit steel. She studied the shot pattern and counted twenty-six holes.

"Hey, Corky," she said. "I think—"

Corky was no longer on the street. He was nowhere in sight.

More cops arrived very quickly, forming a perimeter around the site of the attempted shooting. Several excitable New Yorkers were already giving their personal versions of what had happened. Erin ignored them. She found the highest-ranking cop, a senior sergeant, and told him what she'd seen. Then she walked about thirty yards to the front door of the Barley Corner and went inside.

She was completely unsurprised to see Corky sitting calmly at the bar with Carlyle. She also saw Ian, Caleb, and a couple of rough-looking guys near the door. Ian gave Erin a slight nod. Caleb and the other two goons scowled. All of them looked tense. Carlyle stood up to greet her. Corky remained sitting, looking as relaxed as if he'd been there for an hour.

Erin crossed the room and grabbed Corky's shoulder. "What do you think you're doing?"

"Just having a drink with my mate," he said guilelessly. "You're welcome to join us, love."

"Those guys just tried to kill you!" she snapped.

Corky grinned. "There's no better time for a whiskey than when a lad's come in kissing distance of the old man with the scythe. Besides, love, there were forty people within a quick call of us. Who's to say who those lads were trying to slaughter? I'm an innocent bystander. You'll note I fired no shots."

"You don't carry a gun," she said through clenched teeth. "And I know he was shooting at you because the car we were hiding behind caught practically his whole clip."

"You sure you weren't the target?" Corky asked.

"Are you all right, darling?" Carlyle interjected.

"Of course I am," she said. "You want to worry, worry about this idiot. Tell him to take this seriously."

Carlyle smiled gently. "I've known Corky a sight longer than you, Erin, and I've never known him to take this sort of thing seriously. Was anyone harmed?"

"No. A Ford Fusion went down in the line of duty, that's about it."

"Is this likely to land on your desk?" he asked.

She thought about it and shook her head. "Nobody got hurt, so I don't think so. It'll probably get kicked over to the gang task force. You should tell your boys to calm down and maybe make sure no one's carrying anything that could get them in trouble if they get stopped."

Carlyle nodded. "Corky makes a legitimate point," he said. "This may have been an attempt on you."

"No," Erin said. "I'd only just arrived. That car wasn't following me. I'd have marked a big SUV on my ass. And no one knew I was coming here. Corky was the target."

"It's grand to know someone cares," Corky said, sipping his whiskey.

"What makes you think I care if you get whacked?" she retorted.

"I was talking about the shooter, love," he volleyed back without hesitation.

"I don't suppose you're willing to make a statement," she said.

"I'll make any number of statements, opinions, offers," Corky said. "But I doubt the officer in charge of this craic will be wanting to hear them."

"Do you know who might have done this?" she asked Carlyle.

"I've a number of folk in mind," he said. "But none I'm prepared to swear to. I'll be making my own inquiries, no fear."

"Just try not to start a war," she said.

"The lads who shot first are the ones who started it," he said.

Erin gave him a look. "Be careful, okay? Just because Major Crimes isn't involved now doesn't mean we'll always be on the sidelines. Don't make me come looking for any of your guys."

*   *   *

That was how Erin ended up without her lunch, fishing for food in the unreliable vending machine back at the precinct.

She'd used up her available meal time talking to the other officers at the scene of the attempted shooting, and she hadn't had much appetite anyway, not after the massive jolt of adrenaline. She went upstairs clutching a bag of chips and a Diet Coke.

"You done having fun without me?" Vic asked. He had a Chinese takeout box and a Mountain Dew at his desk. Judging by the wrapper in the trash can, Webb had gone with fast food.

"Oh, you know, just a typical lunch break," Erin said, sliding into her chair. "Talking about suspects, dodging bullets, getting in gunfights."

"Ha ha," Vic said. "Find anything interesting?"

"Not really. Apparently Amelia didn't have any friends. Kept to herself, mostly."

"That's no help," Webb said.

"Maybe not," Erin said thoughtfully. "The professor I talked to said she was a really nice girl."

"You think he was into her?" Vic asked.

"It's not always about sex, Vic," she said.

"It usually is," he said.

"Thank you for that insight into human psychology," Webb said. "Freud would be so proud."

Erin was looking up the background they'd found for Amelia on her computer. "We don't have a next of kin listed," she said.

"There isn't one," Webb said. "Her parents were killed when she was in college. Car crash."

"That's rough," Vic said. "No sisters or brothers?"

"Negative," Webb said.

"That could explain why she was so withdrawn," Erin said. "And why she might have been emotionally vulnerable. Any luck with home invasions, Vic?"

"Hard to say," Vic said. "I mean, I've got a bunch of them on file. Read through this shit and you'll never leave your door unlocked again. You don't even want to know how many people come home and find some asshole sitting in their living room. But none of them match this MO. They steal stuff, or they rape someone, or it's a revenge hit, gang-related. Usually they're after drugs and cash."

"And as far as we know, nothing was taken from the Bledsoe apartment," Erin said. "Why did the killer ransack the place?"

"He did a half-assed job," Vic said. "Only half the place was tossed."

"Which could mean he was looking for something specific," Webb said. "Why keep looking after you've found what you're looking for?"

"Amelia was just a student," Erin said. "Ryan works at a drugstore. You think someone broke in looking for allergy medication?"

"You can cook meth out of allergy medicine," Vic pointed out.

Erin gave him a look. "Yes, Vic, I'm a cop. I know where meth comes from. Are you seriously suggesting Ryan had fifty pounds of allergy meds in his closet?"

"It's unlikely," he admitted. "But I did find a series of break-ins in the area. This guy, a meth-head probably, has been busting in and grabbing pharmaceuticals."

"Does he match the description Bledsoe gave us?" Webb asked.

"White guy, long stringy hair, beard, ratty clothes, dirty," Vic said.

"So, basically the opposite of Curtis Dahl," Erin said.

"So we're trusting Bledsoe's description again?" Vic asked. "Goddamn eyewitnesses. It was almost easier back in the old days, when nobody saw nothin.'"

"Why are you picking out this guy?" Webb asked. "There's got to be dozens of home invasions in Manhattan, like you said."

"He breaks down apartment doors during the day," Vic said. "I've got five witness reports of him coming or going. Plus one of him actually smashing his way in."

"And now you like witnesses again?" Erin asked with a mischievous gleam in her eye.

"Bite me, O'Reilly," Vic said.

"Is he operating in the right neighborhood?" Webb asked.

"Six-block radius of our scene," Vic confirmed.

"Any prior violence against residents?"

"All the other folks were away from home when he hit them," Vic said. "He goes in mid-morning. I talked to the detective on the case. He thinks the guy cases the place, maybe posing as a panhandler, and goes in once they leave for work. Could be he just got unlucky this time."

"We have a name?" Webb asked. "Face?"

"Got a sketch from one of the witnesses," Vic said, rolling his eyes. Like most cops, he knew eerily-accurate composite sketches occupied the realm of fantasy. Sketch artists did their best, but only managed to help with arrests about thirty percent of the time.

"Well, let's have a look," Webb sighed. The three detectives clustered around Vic's computer as he called up the image.

"He looks like the Unabomber," Erin said after a moment.

"Thought of that," Vic said. "The Unabomber's in jail. Florence Supermax, Colorado. He's still there, I think."

The face did resemble the infamous mad bomber, down to the unkempt hair, salt-and-pepper beard, and gaunt, hollow-eyed expression.

"That doesn't help us much," Webb said. "There's got to be a hundred guys on the street who look like that. Manhattan's got a pretty big transient population, and that's assuming the guy's homeless. For all we know, he's a Wall Street broker feeding a drug habit."

"Whether he's our guy or not, somebody better scoop him up," Vic said. "Another place got hit just this morning. Just a block and a half from the Bledsoe place."

"Already?" Webb shook his head. "Doesn't sound like our boy. Why would he hit two places in such rapid succession?"

"Maybe he struck out at the Bledsoes," Erin suggested. "If he didn't find what he wanted there, he'd have tried again."

"There's detectives already working this," Webb said. "You want to horn in on them?"

"Maybe we can do better," Erin said.

"What makes you think so?" Vic asked.

"We've got something they don't," she said with a smile. She snapped her fingers. Rolf hopped to his feet and trotted over to his partner. "Dirty people are easy to track."

* * *

The three detectives, plus Rolf, arrived at the new crime scene to find it taped off and deserted. It was a ground-floor apartment. The door was splintered. It had been rigged with a temporary lock, the hasp screwed into the doorframe.

"Don't know what you'll find," the superintendent said. "The other guys went over it pretty good."

"If you could just let us in, please," Webb said. "We won't be long."

The super unlocked the padlock. The apartment inside was small. Aside from the broken bits of wood from the door, there wasn't much sign of the intruder. Erin, still operating on the assumption they were looking for a junkie, walked straight to the bathroom.

The medicine cabinet door hung askew, one of its hinges broken. Pill bottles were strewn all over the room, a couple lying in the sink, several more on the floor. Erin stooped and indicated one of the fallen bottles.

"Rolf," she said. "*Such!*"

The Shepherd put his nose to the bottle and snuffled at it. He hesitated, tail waving uncertainly. Erin knew he could smell more than one person. She hoped he'd go for the freshest scent.

"Five bucks says he goes after the guy who lives here," Vic said from the doorway.

"You're on," Erin said without looking at him.

Rolf turned and trotted out of the bathroom, tail wagging more enthusiastically. He'd made his decision. He went straight out of the apartment, past the bemused super, down the hall, and out onto Duane Street.

Urban tracking was difficult at the best of times. Concrete and asphalt didn't hold smells as well as more organic surfaces, and the crisscrossing paths of countless New Yorkers could muddle the trail. Then there was always the chance the suspect might just get in a car and drive away, or get on the subway. If that had happened, they were screwed.

But Erin didn't think this guy would do that. By hitting the same neighborhood, over and over, he was showing he probably lived nearby. He sounded like he didn't have much cash, so wouldn't be likely to have a car. The subway was possible, but then the tight radius of targets didn't make much sense.

Rolf, at any rate, was sure of himself. He led the way along Duane Street to West Broadway and turned south. Vic and Webb followed, Webb puffing and wheezing, Vic not even breathing hard.

A block south, at Bogardus Garden, Rolf angled into the park. It wasn't much of a park, really, just a little stand of trees with a few benches. On one of the benches lay a curled-up figure dressed in a ragged gray hooded sweatshirt and tattered jeans. He looked asleep.

Rolf made straight for the huddled man. Erin pulled him up short. The K-9 whined and scratched at the concrete.

"That's him," she said in a low voice.

"Great," Vic muttered. "I love rousting junkies. I'm gonna get a needle stick and get hepatitis or something."

"And you owe me five bucks," Erin added.

"Sir," Webb said loudly. "This is the NYPD."

"Show me your hands!" Vic snapped. The detectives spread out and moved in from both sides, Erin and Rolf from the left, Vic and Webb from the right. Webb drew his revolver. Erin had her hand on her Glock but didn't pull it.

The man didn't react until Vic was right on top of him. The big Russian put out a hand and grabbed the guy's arm. He rotated the arm, spinning the man clean around and down onto the ground in a single fast movement. Vic was almost double the other guy's weight. It wasn't even a contest. The man went down with an exclamation of surprise. By the time Erin and Webb closed in, Vic had the cuffs on him.

"What's your name, punk?" Vic demanded.

"Sic," the guy mumbled. His motions were jerky and twitchy. His pupils were so dilated Erin couldn't even tell what color his eyes were.

"Didn't catch that," Webb said.

"Sick," the man said again. Then he threw up on Vic's shoes.

"I think he meant..." Erin began.

"Yeah," Vic said sourly. "I know what he meant. Thanks."

Chapter 10

While Vic hosed off his footwear back at the precinct showers, Erin fingerprinted their suspect. His prints immediately popped in the database as belonging to Aaron Bosch, age thirty-two. He had a lengthy list of drug offenses, all of them minor. Erin was disgusted, but not surprised, to find the detectives hadn't matched him to any prints from prior crime scenes. Non-violent burglaries just weren't much of a priority to some cops.

They'd stowed Bosch in the interrogation room while they ran him through the system. His pockets had contained a short-handled crowbar, a few odds and ends, and a half-empty bottle of prescription pain meds that had certainly been stolen from the apartment that morning.

"You and me," Vic announced to Erin as he walked into Major Crimes, leaving wet footprints on the concrete.

"The Lieutenant doesn't want to do this one?" Erin asked. Webb usually liked to perform interrogations.

"He said I could use the practice," Vic said. "Whatever that means. Anyway, this guy doesn't seem like he'll be tough to crack. You want to be bad cop this time, just for fun?"

"Vic, he puked on your shoes. I think that makes you bad cop. I'll be good cop."

"You always get to be good cop," he sulked. "Just because I got a little mileage on my face, I've always gotta be the scary guy?"

"Play to your strengths," she said, patting him on the shoulder.

Aaron Bosch greeted them in the interrogation room with the foulest breath Erin had ever smelled off a living man. His teeth were rotten almost down to the gums. Up close, the reek of the guy's unwashed body, which was speckled with skin sores, was indescribable.

"What... what you... want?" he asked, looking from one of them to the other with jittery eyes.

"Just want to know why you killed Amelia Bledsoe," Vic said.

"Don't know... 'Melia... Bless... go..."

"Focus!" Vic shouted.

Bosch gave him a quick, frightened look. "Don't... hurt me," he whimpered. "Not my... fault. Didn't mean... nothing."

"Mr. Bosch," Erin said. "You need help. I want to help you. I just need you to tell me what you've been doing."

"Work... working..."

"What's your job, Mr. Bosch?" She didn't believe it for a second.

"Liveryman."

"Delivery man?" Erin asked.

He nodded.

"What do you deliver?"

"Pills."

"Who do you deliver them to?"

"Guy I... guy I know." Bosch's face twitched suddenly, a sharp spasm. He was shivering, but whether from cold or from nerve damage she couldn't tell.

"Where do you get them?" she asked.

Bosch didn't answer.

"She asked you a question, asshole!" Vic broke in. "Where'd you get the damn pills?"

"Partment. Door... went in..."

"You break the doors down?" Erin asked quietly.

"Give me... give..."

"What do you want, Mr. Bosch?"

"Stuff..."

"Mr. Bosch, tell me what we need to know, and I'll make sure you get what you need."

He looked at her with mingled hope and suspicion. "Need..." he pleaded.

"How do you get into the apartments?" Erin asked.

"Hit... doors," he said.

"With what?"

"You took it... 'way," Bosch whined. "Give it back. It's mine."

"Have you ever hurt anyone?" Erin asked. "In the apartments?"

"No."

"Except the girl in the bathrobe," Vic put in. "You remember her?"

"What... girl?"

"You beat her up and choked her," Vic said. "Don't you remember? Think, you damn meth-head loser!"

"No," Bosch whimpered, raising his cuffed hands in front of his face as if he expected Vic to hit him. "No, I like girls. Nice girl... gave me a dollar... in the park. Yesterday. I think."

"I don't suppose there's any point asking him for an alibi," Erin whispered to Vic. Bosch had buried his head in his hands and appeared to be crying. Sudden mood swings were another symptom of meth abuse.

Vic shook his head. "He's not our guy," he said in disgust.

"No," Erin agreed. She stood up.

"I can... I can go?" Bosch asked hopefully, peering at her between his fingers.

"In seven to ten," Vic said. "With time off for good behavior, maybe. But I doubt it."

*   *   *

"He's not our guy," Erin repeated to Webb. "No gloves, so he would've left prints. No history of violence. And he's got a favorite tool. He wouldn't have left that hammer behind."

"Plus, he's not strong enough," Vic said. "Look at that guy. He's lost a quarter of his weight. He hasn't got any muscle worth mentioning. I'm surprised he could pry a door open. He couldn't strangle a girl, not if she was conscious."

Webb sighed. "You're right. You want to call the Robbery guys and ask them to come collect him?"

"It's better than nothing," Erin said. "He's guilty, just not of killing our victim." She retrieved her half-eaten bag of chips. It had been a long time since her last meal.

"Unfortunately, they don't pay us to solve other peoples' cases," Webb said. "Got any thoughts?"

"I was thinking I'd better take another look at the apartment," Erin said.

"Looking for over-the-counter meds?" Vic asked.

"You're still thinking drugs?" she said. "No, I'm looking for odd socks."

Vic looked confused. "Say what?"

"Things that look wrong."

"Have fun looking through the laundry," Webb said. "I've been looking into Dahl's history and I've got nothing here. He looks like a saint. I haven't seen a single thing in his history that suggests any violent tendencies."

"He was such a nice, quiet man," Vic said. "Kept to himself. No one could have imagined…"

"Point taken, Neshenko," Webb said. "But with killers like this there's almost always a pattern of escalation."

Erin chewed her chips morosely and thought of the Barley Corner's hot, juicy burgers. She stared at her desk, remembering Ryan Bledsoe hammering his fists down on it and shouting. She could still see a stain on the desk. He'd actually left blood there. That was a man who was definitely capable of murderous rage.

She paused and stared at the brown smear. Slowly, she got to her feet.

"Sir," she said quietly.

"What is it, O'Reilly?" Webb asked.

"Can we get a CSU guy in here?"

"Sure," he said. "You want someone to go with you to the apartment?"

"No. I've got some evidence to collect."

"Not at the apartment?"

"No." She pointed to her desk. "The blood on my desk."

"Erin," Vic said, "we don't need a DNA sample from Ryan Bledsoe. It wouldn't do us any good. His DNA is all over his apartment. It's *his apartment*."

"Humor me," she said.

Webb shrugged and reached for the phone.

Erin drove to the Hope Building knowing she was going to find something. She didn't know what yet, but she knew the answer was there. She was feeling the excitement of the chase. Like Rolf on a fresh scent, she was following her nose.

The scene was still sealed. She and Rolf threaded their way through the police tape into the Bledsoe apartment. Everything looked pretty much the way it had the last time she'd seen it. The evidence had been photographed and removed. A fine film of fingerprint powder lay like dust on almost every surface.

Erin reflected that people didn't think about the leftover powder when they thought about "dusting for prints." Her dad had once told her a story about a series of robberies at a car dealership. Crooks had been breaking into new cars to steal the stereo equipment.

"The owner of the dealership kept asking the detectives why they hadn't dusted for prints. They tried to tell him it would make a mess, but he wanted to see his tax dollars at work. He said it'd be okay, he'd just vacuum out the car afterward. So finally, they went ahead and dusted this nice new car. Black powder everywhere. Fast forward a couple weeks, and what do you know? One of the detectives is buying a new car. Guess where he goes? And he takes this nice, clean-looking car out for a test drive. It's a hot day, so he turns on the air conditioner. The moment the air starts flowing, bam! He takes a faceful of fingerprint powder right out of the air vent."

Erin smiled at the memory. Her dad hadn't just been making a joke. He'd been reminding her that actions had consequences and you had to be careful what kind of mess you left behind, because sometimes it came back and blew up in your face.

She scanned the living room, not looking for anything in particular, just letting her eyes wander. They'd been right. This was a weird, half-hearted ransacking. The intruder had knocked over books and a floor lamp, but hadn't done a thorough search. If a guy was serious about looking for hidden contraband, he'd have pulled out the sofa cushions and probably ripped them open. He'd have cut open the upholstery. He'd certainly have checked the fridge. A surprising number of people thought the freezer was a safe place to keep spare cash.

With that thought, she went into the kitchen. She pulled on a pair of disposable gloves, even though CSU had already been through. Better to give in to force of habit than contaminate vital evidence. She opened the freezer. TV dinners, ice trays, frozen vegetables, everything was neatly lined up. There was no sign of a search.

"This wasn't a robbery," she told Rolf, looking back and forth from the kitchen to the living room. "I don't think this guy was searching for anything. It's more like he was just throwing stuff around. Maybe he was still mad, even after killing Amelia?"

But that didn't scan. In Erin's experience, gratuitous violence tended to be visited on the victim, not the surroundings. If the killer still had some pent-up aggression, he'd have just beaten on the victim's body some more. That was why stabbing victims were sometimes stabbed dozens of times.

"Maybe it started out here in the living room," she said, still thinking out loud. "The guy breaks in, Amelia hears him smash the door open, and she confronts him here. They argue, or maybe he's just trying to intimidate her, and he makes a mess to show her he means business? Or there's a struggle?"

Rolf cocked his head, his enormous ears tilting comically to one side. He wanted her to know he was listening.

"Amelia was shy," Erin said, shaking her head. "She was withdrawn, quiet. If she heard someone bust in the door, she wouldn't go out to meet him. She'd hide. And she had her phone with her. Why didn't she call 911? She should've at least had time to dial."

Erin paced off the distance from the front door to the bedroom. If the intruder had been in a hurry and had known where to find her, Amelia might not have had time to call for help. But a stranger wouldn't have known the layout of the apartment, might not have known anyone was home, and certainly wouldn't have known exactly where she was. Amelia should have had at least half a minute, plenty of time to dial the cops. But there had been no 911 call.

"She had to know the killer," Erin said. "We were right about that. That's why she didn't call us. But even if she knew the guy, he still smashed in the door. If somebody did that to my house, I'd call the cops. After I shot him."

Rolf wagged his tail encouragingly. Erin talked to him a lot. He didn't understand most of it, but he liked listening to her.

She stood in the entryway, looking at the broken-in door. "Why a claw hammer?" she asked. "It works, sure, but a sledgehammer is better. Or a crowbar." She peered at the door and frame. It looked like the intruder had hit the area around the knob and lock several times, splintering the wood, and prying the brass lock plate out of the door with the claw end of the hammer.

"That's one hell of an inefficient way to open a door," she told Rolf. "Hell, you could probably just kick it in quicker and easier." She'd done that herself. It was simpler than most people thought, even for an average-sized woman like her. Housebreakers were often crude, but rarely inefficient. They tended to be in a hurry.

"Prying off the lock took time," she said. "Half a minute, maybe? And Amelia would've heard that for sure, unless she was asleep. But she was wearing a bathrobe, so she at least had time to get out of bed." She rubbed her temples. This was giving her a headache. And little flashes of memory kept intruding on her thoughts. She was thinking about the gunman who'd nearly mowed Corky down earlier. That wasn't even her problem. Corky didn't want her help with it, and it wasn't her case.

The hammer. Everything kept coming back to that damned hammer. That was the odd sock. She stared at the carpet where it had been. The hammer, of course, was in the evidence locker back at the Eightball. It just wasn't the tool of a home invader. It was a typical hammer, the sort her dad kept in his toolbox in the garage. Hell, the Bledsoes probably had one of their own lying around. Every household in North America had one, as far as she knew.

Erin opened the hall closet. No signs of looting here. The coats were still on their hangars, the shoes neatly paired with their mates on the floor. Sure enough, a toolbox stood in the corner of the closet. Not sure why she was doing it, just following her stream of consciousness, Erin knelt and unsnapped the lid, opening the box.

The box was one of those that had a lift-out layer with a handle on it. The top layer held a collection of screws, nails, and fasteners. She pulled it out and revealed the main part of the box, where the larger tools were kept. She saw an adjustable wrench, some pliers, some screwdrivers, a tape measure, a fine-toothed handsaw, a carpenter's level, and some other small tools.

She didn't see a hammer.

Erin sat back on her heels and took a deep breath. She remembered more of her dad's advice.

"When things don't make sense, kiddo, you're not looking at them right. Everything makes sense. Always. If the facts don't fit the story, it's the story that's wrong. Start over. Don't assume anything."

Sean O'Reilly hadn't been a detective, but he could've been a great one. Erin knew her father had the eye for it, but he'd never tried hard for the promotion. He'd liked being a Patrol cop, doing the everyday work of policing. He wanted to help people, ordinary people. For him, a shift where he'd gotten a cat out of an old lady's tree was a day well spent.

Erin tried to clear her mind, to look at the scene with fresh eyes. "Start over," she said to Rolf. She closed her eyes. Then, after a moment, she opened them again.

And everything made sense.

"Rolf, *komm!*" she ordered. The Shepherd sprang after her, tail wagging. He could sense her sudden energy and purpose. They left the apartment, hurrying down to the Charger. As they went, Erin dialed her commander.

"Webb," he said.

"I've got it," she said. "I know what happened. Can we get Bledsoe back in?"

"He's going to want to know why," Webb said. "Are we arresting him?"

"We can't. There's not enough proof. But I need to talk to him, face to face."

"Okay," Webb said. "Come on back. I'll call him and tell him we need some follow-up."

"Did CSU swab my desk?" she asked.

"Yeah, they just left."

"Can you tell Levine to put a rush on the bloodwork, sir? We need that sample tested ASAP."

"What's she looking for?"

"Anything that didn't come from Ryan Bledsoe."

Chapter 11

"Did you get the guy?" Bledsoe demanded. He came out of the stairwell full steam, already keyed up and angry.

"Let's step somewhere a little more private and discuss this," Erin said, standing up.

Rolf stood next to her, bristling slightly. He didn't like the feel of this guy.

"What's wrong with right here?" Bledsoe retorted. "Did you get the asshole or didn't you?"

"What we have to talk about might get a little... personal," Erin said, shooting a meaningful look Vic's direction. Vic rolled his eyes and went back to his computer.

"Okay, whatever," Bledsoe said.

Erin led him to the Major Crimes break room. "Do you want to take a seat?" she asked.

Bledsoe looked at his options. He had a choice of two broken-down old kitchen chairs or a very disreputable couch. "I'll stand," he said.

"Coffee?" she offered, closing the door. The two of them and her K-9 were now isolated from the rest of the office. Rolf stuck close to Erin. His hackles were still up. He watched Bledsoe intently.

"No. Thanks," Bledsoe grated out. "Now what did you bring me in here to say?"

"We made an arrest," she said. She drew a cup of espresso for herself and set it on the counter. Then she leaned against the counter and faced him. "Does the name Curtis Dahl mean anything to you?"

"No. Wait, yeah. He's been in the news. His lawyer's saying he was busted just because he's Black. He's the guy?"

"He was in your apartment," Erin said, watching him closely.

"I knew it!" Bledsoe said. "He's the guy from the lobby, isn't he? The one I picked out of the lineup!"

"That's him," she confirmed. "He wasn't a random intruder. He was communicating with Amelia. They were seeing each other often."

A muscle twitched in Bledsoe's jaw. His hands clenched into fists. Erin saw a white bandage on his right hand.

"Are you okay?" she asked, pointing to his hand.

"Huh? Oh, yeah, that happened when I hit your desk. I guess I'm stronger than I thought. Split the skin right open. I didn't even feel it at the time, I was so upset. About my wife."

"I get it," Erin said quietly. "When you're upset, sometimes you can hit a lot harder than you mean to. Did you know Amelia was seeing Curtis?"

"I already told you, I don't know the guy! I didn't know his name!"

"Right," she said. "My mistake. Did you know Amelia was having an affair?"

"She wasn't!" he snapped.

"Are you sure about that?" Erin pressed.

"I would've known!"

"I don't know," she said. "Women can be pretty sneaky when they want to be. I should know."

"What the hell are you talking about? I knew everything my wife got up to. She couldn't have done anything without me finding out."

Erin nodded. "It's funny," she said. "That's not what Curtis told us."

"That jerk doesn't know shit! She was my wife! I knew her!" Bledsoe was really angry now. "He's lying!"

"I thought this might be difficult for you to hear," Erin said in sympathetic tones. "But clearly it wasn't going well. Amelia was scared, so she was breaking off contact with Curtis. Our theory was that he got mad about it and broke the door down."

"Yeah," Bledsoe said, nodding. "He went crazy, I bet. Just totally nuts. Tore up the place, wrecked everything. He's like an animal. You shouldn't have even bothered to arrest him. Too bad he didn't try to run or fight you guys. Would've saved the city some money if you'd just put him down."

"It was a big mess in there," Erin agreed. "The killer pried the plate off the lock to force the door open. He used a hammer to do it. But he threw the hammer away when he got inside. He used his bare hands on Amelia."

"Shut up!" Bledsoe shouted. He pressed his hands against his eyes, as if he was trying to blot out the image in his mind.

"It's hard, thinking about him touching her," she said.

"Shut up! Shut up! You bitch!"

Erin let herself flinch. It went against her training and experience. On the street, working Patrol, you couldn't show weakness or fear. But here, she needed him to see her look scared. She needed to look vulnerable, while still making him mad. It was a tightrope act.

"The thing is, we have a problem," she said. "We don't have evidence of him touching her."

"What?"

"Do you know the principle of transference, Mr. Bledsoe?" she asked.

"What the hell are you talking about?"

"It's the foundation of forensics," she explained. "Whenever anything touches anything else, there's a transfer. Each thing leaves a little of itself on the other thing. Fibers, fingerprints, blood, dirt, everything. But we didn't find anything tying Curtis to your apartment."

"But you said he was there!"

"He was. But we can't prove he was there the day Amelia was killed."

"But I told you, I saw him in the lobby! Are you stupid, or what?"

"When we arrested him at the Guggenheim, he wasn't wearing what you described," she said.

"He must have changed. Afterward."

She nodded. "Maybe he got blood on his clothes. Amelia did bleed, some. The killer probably got blood on himself."

Bledsoe glanced down at his own hands. It was just for an instant, and if she hadn't been looking for it she might have missed it.

"Something's bothering me, though," she went on. "The hammer the killer used to get in. It's the one from the toolbox in your closet."

Bledsoe froze. "I don't know what you're talking about."

"I checked," she said. "But if it's the one from the toolbox, how did he use it to break in?"

"He must have taken it. When he was there. Before. You said he was in the apartment before."

Erin shook her head. "No, that doesn't make sense. This was a crime of passion. For him to take it, he would have to have known ahead of time what he was going to do. Besides, Curtis works setting up art exhibits. He's got access to all kinds of tools. He wouldn't need yours."

"Then he was trying to set me up!" Bledsoe said. "He wanted to make it look like I did it!"

"I don't understand," Erin said. "You had keys to the apartment. Why would you break into your own apartment?"

"So it would look like he did it. Because he wanted it to look like I was setting him up!"

Erin blinked. "That's crazy."

"I'm not crazy, you dumb bitch!" he shouted.

"Aren't you?" she snapped back. "You found out your wife was talking to someone. She wasn't having an affair, not really. She was doing something worse. She was making a friend. A real, close, personal friend. And you just couldn't stand that, could you?"

"Shut up!" His fists were clenched again.

"She was all alone until you found her. She'd lost her parents, she had no other family. She could be all yours. And you're a man who guards his property. But she wasn't a thing, you dumb meathead! She was a person! And when you confronted her, maybe you didn't mean to kill her. Maybe you just wanted to slap some sense into her. You'd done it enough times before."

"That's a goddamn lie!" he shouted at her. The room felt very small. Ryan Bledsoe wasn't a big guy, but he was very angry and Erin was very conscious of his close proximity. She'd been around plenty of violent men in her career. This guy was primed to go off at any moment. Usually, that meant it was time to try to de-escalate the situation, calm everyone down. Not this time. Now it was time to set him off.

"You saw her phone history," she went on. "Amelia had been deleting her messages, but this time she slipped up and left a few and you saw them right before you left for work. You went through all her things, looking for proof of an affair. That's why only her dresser was emptied, not yours. You lost your temper and you hit her, again and again. It felt good. It makes you feel good, hitting someone smaller and weaker than you. You're just a bully who likes to feel strong."

"Shut up! Shut up, shut up, shut up!" He grabbed her by the collar of her blouse with both hands, screaming right in her face. Flecks of spittle sprayed her cheeks.

Erin had been waiting for it. She snapped her head forward, in a street move that would've made Corky stand up and cheer, and head-butted Bledsoe squarely in the nose.

He let go of her and stumbled back. Blood squirted from his nostrils. He clapped a hand to his face and stared at her through watering eyes. Rolf growled at him, but stayed at Erin's side. He hadn't been ordered to attack, and it didn't look to him like there was a fight going on.

"You left Amelia's blood on my desk," Erin said with slow, deliberate triumph. "You thought you'd hide the fact that you hurt your hands by hitting my desk. It was a good trick, but you got bits of her on you, and you left them on my desk. Like I said, it's the principle of transference. And you staged a break-in, but you used a tool from inside your apartment. When we check the hammer, we'll find your DNA on it. You put on gloves when you used the hammer, but not when you used it in the past. We'll prove it was yours. And you just assaulted a police officer. Ryan Bledsoe, you're under arrest for the murder of Amelia Bledsoe. You have the right to remain—"

"Shut up, you mouthy fucking bitch!" he screamed. He lunged at her.

Erin neatly sidestepped, letting his fist swing past her face. She grabbed the extended arm and pulled, increasing his momentum. He overbalanced and crashed against the break room's Formica countertop. The breath whooshed out of him and he doubled over.

Erin stepped behind him and pulled out her cuffs. "You have the right to remain silent," she said, picking up where she'd left off. "Anything you say—"

"I'll kill you, too!" Bledsoe wheezed. His wildly groping hand found Erin's cup of coffee. He flung it over his shoulder, right at her head.

She barely had time to close her eyes before the hot, dark fluid splashed into her face. She cried out and tried to wipe it away. It wasn't quite boiling, but was hot enough to burn. Through the blur of heat and pain, she saw Bledsoe's outline, coming around on her.

"Rolf! *Fass!*" she cried out.

It was all the Shepherd had been waiting for. He coiled his powerful hind legs and sprang. His jaws snapped shut with a sharp clicking sound. A second later, Bledsoe started to scream.

Vic had started for the break room the moment he heard the scuffle. Webb, older and slower, was a few steps behind him. By the time the big Russian burst into the room, Erin and Rolf had Bledsoe down on the floor and Erin was finishing cuffing the man's hands behind his back. Bledsoe's right arm was bleeding from Rolf's fangs, but he wasn't badly hurt.

"That go about like you thought it would?" Vic asked with a sardonic smile.

"Pretty much," Erin grunted, standing up and grabbing some napkins. She swiped her face more or less clean. "Except for the part where he tried to blind me."

"You get what you were looking for?"

"Yeah." She pointed to the corner of the room, where her phone, unnoticed by Bledsoe, had been busily recording the entire sequence of events. "Does 'I'll kill you, too' count as a confession?"

Webb peered around Vic's massive torso into the room. "Yeah, I think that'll help our case," he said. "Good work, O'Reilly. Are you okay?"

"I'm fine. You should see the other guy."

"I'm looking at him," Vic said appreciatively. "You kicked his ass, Erin."

"With a little help," she said, ruffling Rolf's fur.

Rolf wagged his tail. His mouth fell open and his tongue lolled out in an unmistakable smile. But the hair on his neck was still standing on end.

Chapter 12

Booking Bledsoe, and taking care of the corresponding paperwork, took most of the rest of the afternoon. Erin didn't really mind. She needed a couple hours to drain off the adrenaline from the fight in the break room. After they got Bledsoe securely squared away, the detectives went back upstairs.

Vic was amused by the whole thing. "You sure you needed the dog?" he asked. "Try that in the ring, it'll get you disqualified."

"Fighting fair is fighting stupid," Erin replied. That was something else her dad had told her.

"Okay," he said. "But in that case, why stop with the mutt? Why not bring me in, too? I wouldn't have minded taking a couple of shots at him."

"If you'd been there, he wouldn't have tried it," she said. "He needed to think he had a chance if it came to a fight. I wanted to make him lose his cool."

"You succeeded. How's the face?"

"I'm fine." The coffee had hurt, but hadn't been quite hot enough to raise blisters. Her cheeks might be a little tender for a day or two, but she'd had worse.

"A perp attacking an officer in the Eight with her own cup of coffee." Webb sighed and shook his head. "That's a new low, I think. Hanging's too good for him."

"Was that a joke, sir?" Vic asked, feigning surprise.

"Do I tell jokes?" Webb replied, flat deadpan.

Vic and Erin looked at him for a second, trying to decide. Webb's poker face gave nothing away.

"We got anything else in the pipeline?" Vic asked after the moment had spun itself out.

"Not at the moment," Webb said. "There's something cooking with the organized crime squad, but it's not a Major Crimes issue yet."

"What's that?" Erin asked, a little too quickly.

"What, you didn't get enough action today?" Vic asked.

"Apparently someone took a shot at an O'Malley associate outside our old friend Carlyle's establishment," Webb said, reading off his computer screen. "Emptied an assault rifle at him on a crowded street. By some miracle, no one was wounded, let alone killed. We had officers on scene, but the shooter got away clean. Looks like it was a drive-by. One of the officers returned fire. Looks like it was..." He paused.

Erin winced inwardly. She knew what was coming.

Webb looked up from his monitor. "Something you'd like to tell us, O'Reilly?"

Vic also turned toward her. Even Rolf cocked his head at her.

"I told you I was dodging bullets over lunch," she said. "It's not my fault you didn't believe me."

"I thought you were joking!" Vic protested.

"Just answer me this," Webb said wearily. "What were you doing there?"

"I was looking for a hamburger," she said, honestly enough. "Then the bad guys showed up and started spraying bullets. I grabbed cover and shot back. Nobody was hit on either side. That's it."

"Hmm," Webb said noncommittally. "You know anything more about this?"

"The target was James Corcoran, I think," she said. "I ran him down afterward, but he wouldn't make a statement. He seemed to think it was funny."

"Only because they missed," Vic said. "Who do you think the shooters were?"

"No idea. Best guess, Northern Irish militants."

"Like I said, it's not our problem," Webb said. "Not yet, at any rate. So don't sweat it. We've just got one more piece of housekeeping before we call it a day. I'd like a volunteer to drop in on Mr. Dahl and apologize."

Vic rolled his eyes. "Did we hurt his feelings?"

"We arrested the wrong guy, Neshenko," Webb said coldly. "The man's got aggressive legal representation. He's probably considering suing the city. No, I don't care if we hurt his feelings, but we do owe him this much. Given your reaction, I'm giving this one to O'Reilly."

"I thought you wanted a volunteer," Erin said.

"Thank you for volunteering," Webb said. "You can head home afterward. Thanks for taking care of this."

"Yes, sir," she said. She knew an order when she heard it. And Webb was right; they did owe Dahl, and she was a much better person than Vic for this kind of job.

*   *   *

According to the information Erin had, Dahl was back at work. Accordingly, she drove to the Guggenheim. She and Rolf went back into the strange, spiral-shaped building. This time, they talked to one of the employees. The woman checked Erin's credentials, then led her through a service door into the basement.

They found Curtis Dahl at his desk in a windowless office, staring at a floor plan of the museum. He looked up. When he saw Erin, his face froze into a wary mask.

"I can't discuss anything without my lawyer," he said immediately.

She held up a hand. "Mr. Dahl... Curtis, please. This will only take a moment. I'm sorry for bothering you again. I just wanted to apologize for the inconvenience you've been caused, and to assure you that you won't be troubled any further."

"I don't understand."

"We've made an arrest," she said. "And we have a confession. We've got the man who killed Amelia."

She watched a complicated mix of emotions struggle behind Dahl's eyes. "I'm glad to hear that," he said cautiously.

"It was Ryan," she said. "Her husband. He was abusing her. Things finally got out of hand."

"I know that," Dahl said, looking down. "I saw some of the bruises on her. I wanted... I wanted to help her. I tried to tell her to leave him, to get some help."

"Why didn't you tell us you suspected him?" she asked.

"You wouldn't have listened to me," he said bitterly. "You had the guy you wanted. You just would have thought I was trying to throw the blame onto someone else to save myself. And he's the guy who identified me."

"I'm sorry that's what you think," Erin said quietly. She had thought Dahl was guilty, just like the rest of the detectives.

Would she have believed him without more proof of innocence? She'd never know.

"Can I ask you something, ma'am?" Dahl asked, meeting her eyes again.

"Sure."

"Why did he do it? Was it," he paused, "because of me?"

"It wasn't your fault," Erin said firmly. "He did it because he wanted Amelia not to have anyone except him in her life. No friends, no family. He was a controlling jerk. He was a bomb waiting to go off. Something would've set him off, sooner or later. This isn't on you. It's on him. And he's going down for it."

Dahl nodded. "Maybe I'm supposed to feel good about it, but I don't. It's all such a waste, such a stupid waste. Amelia was a good person. She deserved something better. It's not fair and it's not worth it."

"No," Erin said. "It's not. It'll have to be enough."

"Revenge isn't enough," Dahl said. "Not ever."

"Maybe not. But sometimes it's all we can get. I hope it's justice more than revenge."

"What's the difference?"

Erin thought about that. "I guess revenge is if you do something just for yourself, to make yourself feel better. Justice isn't personal."

"Maybe it should be," Dahl said.

Erin smiled slightly, a sad smile. "Maybe you're right," she said. She stepped toward him and extended her hand. "I'm sorry we couldn't do more. Thanks for your time, Mr. Dahl."

"Thanks for coming down here, ma'am," he said, taking her hand. His hand was gentle, warm. Erin wondered how she could ever have thought he was a murderer. "I'm working on an upcoming exhibit. It'll open in May. You should come see it."

"What is it?" she asked, bending forward to peer at his desk.

"It's called 'A Year with Children,'" he said. "It's a collection of art created by students from New York elementary schools. They've been working on projects through our artist-in-residence Learning through Art program."

"Really? I thought you guys just did... you know, famous people."

Dahl smiled. "Every artist starts somewhere."

"I'll try to come," Erin said. "My brother's got a couple of kids. Maybe we can do a family visit."

"That's a good idea," he said. "Amelia... she told me coming here was like stepping outside. Breathing fresh, clean air. I'd like to think this museum was where she felt the most freedom. Maybe there's a part of her still here. If there is, she'd like this. It's bright colors, collages, paintings... all happiness and light."

"Happiness and light," Erin repeated. "Yeah, I think we could all use some of that. Have a good day, Mr. Dahl."

* * *

Erin and Rolf climbed the stairs out of the basement and went back through the service door into the lobby. Erin was feeling better than she had. Her phone buzzed. Glancing down at it, she saw an unknown number. That meant either a scam or a call from Carlyle. He regularly cycled through burner phones. She smiled at his paranoia and lifted the phone.

"Erin?"

The voice, just in front of her, made her freeze in place. The phone, still buzzing, was suspended just below her ear. In front of her stood a man who reminded her of a J. Crew catalog ad, from his neatly combed hair through his polo shirt and slacks down to his well-shined shoes.

"Luke?" she said in disbelief.

"It's nice to see you remember me," Luke Devins said, but his smile was a little uncertain. He and Erin hadn't seen each other since he'd broken up with her almost a year ago. That had also been in an art gallery, right after Erin had retrieved a stolen Renaissance painting. Luke was an art appraiser, a good, decent, helpful guy who just hadn't been able to stomach dating a cop. Not everyone could.

"I wouldn't forget you," she said.

"You're working, I see," he said, pointing to Rolf. "More art thieves?"

"Who's this, Luke?" the woman beside him asked.

Erin's attention shifted to her. Luke's companion was clearly a society woman, dark hair intricately styled, chic blouse and skirt, gym-toned olive-skinned body and great complexion. This woman was prettier than Erin was, not least because she obviously spent a lot of time and money making herself that way. The woman laid a hand on Luke's arm in a subconsciously possessive way.

"Esme, this is Erin O'Reilly," Luke said. "You remember, I told you about her? The police officer?"

The woman's full, beautiful lips parted in a dazzling smile, showing perfect rows of bright white teeth. "Yes, of course! Officer O'Reilly, it's a pleasure to meet you. Esmeralda Dominguez. My friends call me Esme." She extended a well-manicured hand.

Erin shook. "It's Detective O'Reilly, actually. Pleasure's mine." The phone buzzed again, distractingly. Unsure where to direct her attention, she let it ring.

"And this must be..." Esmeralda said, indicating Rolf.

"Rolf," Luke said. "I remember him." He offered the K-9 his hand, which the Shepherd sniffed in a professional manner. "How've you been, Erin?"

"SSDD," she said. Her phone gave one last plaintive buzz and fell silent.

Luke and Esmeralda looked blank. "I'm sorry?" he said.

"Same shit, different day."

Esmeralda laughed. She had a musical, charming laugh. "That's the human condition, Detective. Or should I call you Erin?"

"This is a social meeting," Erin said. "Erin's fine. If I arrest you, then you can call me Detective."

Esmeralda laughed again. "I can see why Luke liked you." She threaded her fingers through Luke's and drew in next to him. "I always thought police officers were bald, humorless men."

"That's my dad you're thinking of," Erin said with a smile. "How'd you two meet?"

"At an art exhibition, of course," Esmeralda said.

"Raphael?" Erin guessed.

"Dominguez," Luke said, giving Esmeralda a warm look.

"You're a painter?" Erin asked.

Esmeralda nodded. "I know Luke mostly goes for artists who are a little older than I am. But he made an exception in my case."

"She's got an extraordinary eye and hand," Luke said. "I think she's going places."

"Do you have anything on display here?" Erin asked, gesturing around the Guggenheim's lobby.

"No," Esmeralda said. "We're here for the display on Italian Futurism."

"Like, spaceships and stuff?" Erin asked.

Esmeralda laughed again. Erin found it less charming this time. She hadn't meant it as a joke.

Luke, seeing her confusion, stepped in. "It was an early twentieth-century movement in Italy that emphasized technology, youth, speed, and unfortunately violence. It looked forward into the last century and did a pretty good job predicting some of the major social movements. Sadly, it's most associated with Fascism. The Futurists thought Mussolini would modernize the country. When he went down, he took the Futurist movement with him."

"Good riddance," Erin said. "Why are you interested in Nazi art?"

"Fascist, not Nazi," Luke said. Then he raised a hand. "Okay, okay, that's an academic distinction. But I actually started paying attention to the artistic movements around World War II because of the Orphans of Europe exhibit, the looted Nazi artwork we went to see together. I started wondering how the old masters interacted with the newer artists, looking for unifying threads. My heart's still with the Renaissance masters. I guess going to a Futurist exhibit is sort of the artistic equivalent of watching a horror movie for me."

"Luke, I think her eyes are glazing over," Esmeralda said.

It was Erin's turn to laugh. "No, it's okay. It's interesting stuff. I'm glad you're keeping busy, Luke."

"So are you," he said. "I keep reading about you in the paper. You're kind of famous."

"I wouldn't know," she said. "I don't read about myself."

Her phone began buzzing again. It was the same number. "I'd better take this," she said. "It might be important."

"Don't let us keep you," Luke said. "Be careful, Erin. I still worry about you sometimes."

"That's sweet of you," she said. "But I'll be fine. It's the other guys you should worry about."

She nodded farewell to Luke and his new girl as she turned away and answered the phone.

"O'Reilly."

"Erin, darling," Carlyle said. "I'm glad I was able to get through to you."

"Everything okay?" she asked.

There was a short pause, which opened wide enough for all kinds of worries to pour into the gap.

"I'm needing to take a bit of a trip," Carlyle said, sidestepping the question. "Would you care to come away with me for a few days?"

"We just had a vacation," she reminded him.

"I didn't say a vacation."

"Where are you going?"

"Down to the Bahamas. I'll be traveling by private jet."

"That sounds like a vacation to me. What's going on? Why the short notice?"

"A few things have been happening here," he said. "I'm sure you'll hear about them on your end. Evan and I agreed it's best Corky and I step away from New York for a short while. It'll give everyone a chance to calm down."

"I'm not going on a three-way vacation with you and Corky."

"Nay, Corky's traveling separately. He'll be in another country altogether. Mexico, I'm thinking."

"Oh." Erin's thoughts were racing. "Look, give me a straight answer. What happened?"

"I'd prefer not to go into the details over the phone."

"God damn it, Carlyle, what did you do?" It was fear that gave an edge to her voice, but it sounded just like anger. Erin wasn't entirely sure which emotion was on top.

"It doesn't matter what I've done. What matters is how it appears. And right now, it appears I'm involved in the disappearance of some lads formerly connected with the Ulster Volunteer Front."

"The UVF? You mean those guys who got shot in Belfast?"

"Mates of theirs. In New York."

"Christ. Were those the guys who tried to get Corky?"

"In all likelihood. You understand the appearance of the thing now, I take it?"

She could. Whatever had happened to the UVF goons, everyone in the New York underworld would assume it was something to do with Carlyle and Corky, retaliation for their attack on Corky. Erin closed her eyes and tried to stay calm. She couldn't escape the thought that Carlyle very well might have had something to do with this. He wasn't a muscle guy, she reminded herself. He handled money and gambling contacts for the O'Malleys. He didn't whack rivals, or have men killed.

How sure was she of that?

"I'll come with you," she said slowly, "on one condition."

"What's that?"

"You tell me, truthfully, you had nothing to do with these guys disappearing."

"I've never lied to you, darling. And I'd nothing to do with it, as God's my witness."

She let out a breath she didn't know she'd been holding. "Okay. When are you leaving?"

"This evening. From the charter terminal at JFK, at eight o' clock."

"That's less than three hours from now. You expect me to drop everything, just like that?"

"I'm expecting nothing, darling. But I'm asking."

"Okay. Let me make a couple of calls. How warm is it down there?"

"It's the Bahamas, darling. Sun and surf. Pack a bathing suit."

"Rolf's coat is a little too heavy for that. I'll call my brother, see if they can take him. How long will we be gone?"

"A week at most. This won't be like in the movies, darling. We're just getting a bit of space."

"All right. I'll see you at the airport."

"Grand."

Erin hung up and stared at the phone. Rolf, at her side, was watching her intently, his brown eyes unreadable.

"What the hell am I doing?" she asked him.

Rolf wagged his tail. He didn't know, but that didn't bother him. He'd given up on understanding everything humans did.

Chapter 13

Michelle took Erin's call and said she'd have to consult with her family about taking Rolf for a few days. Erin waited while Michelle consulted. Anna's squeal of joy was clearly audible over the phone.

"Sure thing," Michelle said. "Do you have time to drop him off, or should I come get him?"

"I have to get to JFK," Erin said. "Why don't you come by the apartment? You can let yourself in. I'll leave Rolf's food and leash by the door." Sean Junior had a spare key to Erin's place for exactly this sort of situation.

"What's the big rush?" Michelle asked. "Where are you going?"

"Last-minute personal trip."

There was a short pause. Then Michelle said, "Your boyfriend's flying you to Paris, isn't he."

"Well... no."

"Rome?"

"No."

"Tahiti? Hawaii? New Zealand? I can keep guessing."

"The Bahamas."

"Seriously? Sis, you better nail this guy down and marry him."

"Shelley, I don't think... that is, I'm not..."

"Do you love him?"

"Yes."

"Does he love you?"

"Yes."

"What's the problem?"

"It's not who he is, it's what he is, and you know it."

"You still think your dad won't accept him?"

"I think Dad might shoot him on sight."

"Oh. Well, that would put a crimp on wedding rehearsal day."

"Shelley, I have to go. I've got some plans still to make and some packing to do."

"Have you got a sexy bikini?"

"Shelley!"

"Because you've got the body for it. I'm just saying. Not every woman in her thirties can say that."

"I'll call you when I get back, Shelley. My love to Sean and the kids."

"Be good, Erin." Michelle paused, and Erin could imagine the sparkle in her sister-in-law's eye. "But not too good."

Then it was time to call Webb. She had to think what she was going to tell him. He was a very experienced detective who could smell bullshit even over a phone line.

"Webb."

"Evening, sir. It's O'Reilly. I'm sorry for the short notice, but I need to take a few personal days. Something unexpected has come up, some family business that needs to be taken care of. I'll be out of town for about a week. Is that going to be a problem?"

Webb thought about it. "No, we should be okay. It's good we got the Bledsoe thing wrapped up. It's not anything too serious, is it? The family's okay?"

Erin was surprised he cared. Webb didn't usually express the slightest concern, or even interest, in his detectives' families. Nor his own, come to that. She knew he was twice divorced, with a couple of teenage kids living with their mom out in California.

"Everyone's okay, sir. It's not an emergency, just something I need to do."

"All right. Be sure to log the time off when you get back. And keep your phone with you, in case we need to reach you."

"I'll be out of state."

"We still may need to talk to you. I promise not to disturb you unless it's earth-shattering."

"Thank you, sir."

With that out of the way, Erin needed to pack. Fortunately, she wasn't one of those women who had to spend all day sorting out her wardrobe. She thought of Esmeralda, Luke's new girl, with a dash of contempt. That woman looked like she took an hour getting dressed every morning. Erin gave Rolf a quick turn around the block, then got down to looking at her clothes. She laid out summer outfits, mostly T-shirts and tank tops, shorts, a pair of slacks and a nice blouse in case they went out somewhere fancy for dinner. She packed her running shoes and a pair of comfy walking shoes, along with some sandals. She didn't actually own a bikini, so in spite of Michelle's advice, she packed the only swimsuit she had, a black one-piece. A couple of baseball caps, some socks and underwear, and her toiletries, and she was pretty much set.

She checked the clock. She had an hour and a half to make it to JFK. She'd have to hurry. Fortunately, getting on a charter flight didn't require the same hefty lead time as a commercial airliner. She thought about bringing some booze, but laughed it off. Carlyle would definitely have something on the plane, and the Bahamas were famous for good cheap liquor. This would be a good chance to drink rum, if nothing else.

Rolf, standing in the bedroom doorway, gave her a soulful, reproachful stare. He knew what a suitcase meant.

"Don't give me that," she said. "You'll have a great time with Anna and Patrick. Give me a wag now."

Rolf's tail stayed stubbornly still, tucked low. He ducked his head and looked sadly up at her.

"Good boy, Rolf," she said, scratching his head. "*Sei brav.*"

That got a slight, sulky motion of the tail. It would have to do.

Erin put out Rolf's things where Michelle would see them. Was she forgetting anything? She looked around the apartment one more time.

Then she thought of her guns. This was part vacation, part escape. It seemed unlikely they'd be attacked in the Caribbean. But being caught unarmed if things went sideways would be unforgivable. She wavered. Finally, she decided to just bring her snub-nosed .38 revolver. It was small, light, and compact. She could carry it without attracting attention. She left her Glock in her closet in its holster, strapped the .38 to her ankle, and went out the door.

Since she didn't have Rolf to worry about, she took a taxi to JFK. That would save time and money on parking. The cabbie got her to the airport with a little less than forty minutes to spare. She flashed her shield to the TSA folks and hurried inside, calling the number Carlyle had used to contact her as she went.

"Evening, darling," he said.

"I'm here. Where are you?"

"Look around. Ian's standing watch for you."

Erin turned around. Sure enough, there was Ian Thompson, less than twenty yards away. He nodded politely.

"Ma'am."

"How do you sneak up like that?" she demanded. "That's a little creepy."

"Sorry, ma'am. No excuse."

Somehow, she'd known he'd say that. "You know where we're going?" she asked.

"Follow me, ma'am."

Ian led her to the gate, where a King Air C90 was waiting. Erin stared at it.

"That's the smallest plane I've ever seen," she said.

"Six-seater twin-piston turboprop," Ian said. "I've flown on smaller ones."

"As I recall, one of those crashed into a mountainside."

"It was shot down, ma'am. I don't expect to take ground fire on this op."

"That's a relief. So you're coming with us?"

"Affirmative, ma'am. I'll stay out of the way."

"Anyone else coming along?"

"Mr. Carnahan is flying. And there's a co-pilot."

"Caleb's a pilot?"

Ian nodded. "Fully qualified."

That told Erin the flight crew would be all Carlyle's guys. They were taking the threat of the UVF seriously. Ian offered to take her bag. Erin refused. He didn't press the issue; in the Marine Corps, everyone carried their own duffels. His luggage was apparently already stowed.

Erin climbed into the little propeller plane, wondering if it could possibly get them all the way to the Caribbean. Inside, she saw that the usual six seats had been reconfigured to just four, two facing each way. Carlyle was sitting in one, clad in a cream-colored suit she'd never seen before. He stood to greet her, though the cabin roof was too low to stand fully upright.

"Thanks for coming, Erin. I'm glad."

"This should be fun," she said. "I see you busted out your tropical wardrobe."

"Aye. Here's to a pleasant journey. May the good saints protect us and bless us today, and may troubles ignore us each step of the way."

"Old Irish blessing?"

He smiled. "Aye. Would you be wanting something to drink?"

"Once we're in the air. I remember one time at this airport, a charter flight didn't get off the ground. Some crazy bastard drove a car on the runway to stop it."

Carlyle's smile broadened. "Would you be knowing the crazy bastard in question?"

"Yeah, that was Vic." Erin sat down and buckled her seatbelt. "I've never ridden in a propeller plane before."

"It's a smooth enough ride," Carlyle said. "Relax and enjoy the journey."

Ian took one of the remaining seats, the one facing the door. He pulled a flat black case out from under the seat and held it in his lap. Somehow, Erin didn't think it was full of tropical clothing. Like her, he wouldn't relax until they had a few thousand feet of air between them and whatever trouble Carlyle was leaving behind.

* * *

If she had to go on the run from paramilitary hit men, Erin reflected, the Bahamas were a pretty nice place to lie low. It was like living in a postcard. The colors, especially the greens and blues, were deeper and brighter than anything she remembered from New York. She and Carlyle spent their days swimming, walking on the beaches, touring the small shops in the nearby town, sitting in the sun, and sipping cold drinks. She tried the local rum, of course, and liked it. They had cocktails, too. Both of them tried something called a "first love," a sweet cocktail mixed with gin and cherry liqueur. At night, they went dancing, or just talked.

Ian was always there, in the background, but he was careful not to intrude. He drifted nearby, close enough so he could take action if needed. Like Erin and Carlyle, he'd changed into beach attire, but it didn't matter what Ian Thompson wore. He always looked like a Marine. Light slacks and a Hawaiian shirt didn't fool anybody, especially since Erin could see the bulge of his Beretta under his shirttail and the long, intricate tattoo running up his left arm.

"What's the story behind Ian's ink?" she asked Carlyle on the third night. They were on the grass just above the beach. She was lying on her back, her head pillowed against his leg.

"What makes you think there's a story?" he replied in classic Carlyle style, blocking a question with another question.

"It's a tattoo. There's always a story. Even if the story's just about getting drunk and thinking it was a good idea."

"The lad had part of it done on his first tour, in Iraq," Carlyle said. "He got the rest in Afghanistan, except for a wee bit near the wrist. He acquired that upon his return. He's never told me what it signifies."

"I can't make all of it out," she said. "It looks like Bible stories, from what I can see."

"Does that surprise you, darling?"

"He doesn't seem like a very religious guy."

"He's a lad who values dedication to duty," Carlyle said. "If he'd not been a soldier, perhaps he'd have made a fine monk."

That startled a laugh out of her. "Really?"

"He's unmarried and Catholic. Those are the principal qualifications."

"Has he ever had a girlfriend?"

"Oh aye, there was a lass back in high school. A fine colleen by the name of Amanda. Unfortunately, that didn't last through his first deployment."

"No one since then?"

"Not to my knowledge."

Erin considered. "That was years ago. Doesn't the poor guy ever get laid?"

"If he does, I'm not the one he tells about it. Not that he'd share that sort of information, particularly with me. Do you talk to your da about your love affairs?"

She shuddered. "Of course not!" Then, remembering her conversation with Michelle, she became more quiet and thoughtful.

"You're thinking about the future," Carlyle said gently.

"How can you tell?"

"You get worried. You've a particular expression on your face."

She managed a weak chuckle. "Well, yeah. Thing is, either we're going to break this off someday, or Dad's going to find out sooner or later. Or..."

"Or the matter will be otherwise arranged for," he said softly. "What is it you want, Erin?"

"I don't want to hide," she said. "I don't want to lie. I'm not ashamed of you. You're a good man. Well, mostly."

It was his turn to laugh. "I'll choose to take that as a compliment, darling."

"I ran into an old boyfriend, the day we left," she said.

"Aye?"

"Yeah. He was with his new girl."

"What did you make of her?"

"Oh, she's a knockout. Gorgeous, friendly. Perfect."

"You're a fair treat yourself, darling."

"Thanks."

"Did it bother you? Seeing him with another lass?"

"No. Well, yeah. A little. But not because... I wasn't jealous of her. Not really. I guess maybe I was jealous of them. Together. They could just walk down the street, hand in hand, and no one would take a shot at them, or fire them. They were ordinary. Safe."

"And that's what you're wanting, Erin? Ordinary and safe?"

"What do you think?"

"I think you're fond of adventure. I think you prefer a lad who's interesting, and perhaps a bit dangerous."

Erin nodded. "Can I ask you something?"

"You can always ask."

"But you'll dodge if you don't want to answer."

"That goes without saying, darling."

"If you could go back in time, to when you first came over from Ireland, and make different choices, would you?"

"You mean, would I still throw in with Evan O'Malley?"

"Yeah."

Carlyle thought about it. Erin listened to the rhythmic pulse of the waves as they rolled onto the beach.

"I would," he said at last.

"You'd still want to be a gangster?"

"I never wanted to be a gangster."

"I don't understand. Why go through the same shit, if you didn't have to?"

He laid a hand on the side of her face, caressing her cheek. "Because if I'd chosen a different life, I'd likely never have met you. You're worth all of it, Erin. The good and the bad."

"That's sweet. But you could've become a cop, maybe."

He laughed. "Now there's a thought! But the truth is, Erin, we can't change the path we're on. We certainly can't rip it up and start over."

"That UVF guy who got killed," Erin said. "The guy in Ireland. Do you think he's the one who shot your wife?"

Carlyle sighed. "I've no idea. I think it's likely, though."

"Why do you say that?"

"Because Siobhan wouldn't have done it that way if she didn't think so."

Erin levered herself to a sitting position so she could look Carlyle in the eye. "Why did she?"

"I imagine it was her idea of a present. Or a message."

"Aimed at you?"

"Aye."

"But she thought you betrayed her. When she was here last."

"I did betray her, Erin, in case you've forgotten," he said with a hint of sharpness that made her flinch. "But in spite of that, she still loves me. We're family, she and I."

"That girl's all kinds of screwed up."

"I fear you're right about that, darling. Still, I'd wager I could talk some sense into her, given the chance."

"Maybe," Erin said doubtfully. "But if I'm worried what my dad would think of you, I'm even more worried what Siobhan thinks of me. Wicked stepmother wouldn't even begin to describe it. Have you heard from her?"

"Not since she left the Barley Corner," he said. "Not a word. I'd no notion she was even in Belfast. She's likely moved on from there, to some old Brigade bolt-hole I'd warrant." He smiled sadly. "We're all of us hiding from something now."

"Carlyle?"

"Aye, darling?"

"What happened to the UVF guys in New York?"

"I don't know for certain."

"But you suspect something."

"Aye. But I can't tell you my suspicions."

Erin knew what he meant by that. He meant his personal code of loyalty forbid him from saying what he thought. That meant two things: he was pretty sure the men who'd tried to kill Corky were now dead, and he was equally sure they'd been killed by someone in the O'Malleys, quite possibly Corky himself. She tried to imagine Corky, with his constant smile and ready laugh, his sparkling eyes and reckless charisma, as a killer. It was difficult, but not impossible.

Then the thought struck her that if a couple of bodies turned up, the case might land on Major Crimes. What would she do if she had to investigate Corky? Could she arrest him?

At that moment, more than any other in her life, Erin didn't want to think like a cop. She was sorry she'd even brought it up. "Let's go inside," she said. "Get me some rum and help me forget all this shit."

"Is that an order, darling?"

"Yeah. You got a problem with that?"

"I'm a publican. I've made a business of helping the Irish forget their troubles. It's why the good Lord gave us liquor. And He gave us hangovers to prevent the Irish from conquering the world."

"Forget the hangover." She stood up and went inside with him.

She closed the door and slid the deadbolt home. Carlyle was pouring her a glass of rum in the living room. She took the glass, gulped the contents into her mouth, dropped the glass, and shoved her mouth against his. Alcohol trickled down her chin and she tasted the drink and the indefinable taste of him. Then his arms were around her, holding her tightly, and she lost herself in him, throwing away all her worries and every thought of the future. She threw him down on the braided rug, right there on the living room floor, with the window open and the smell of the ocean wafting into the room, and straddled him. He let her do it, recognizing her need to take control of something here and now. She might worry again tomorrow, but tonight he was hers.

Chapter 14

Caleb Carnahan had flown the Beechcraft to Miami, where he and his copilot had awaited further instructions. They returned to the Bahamas in the early afternoon of the sixth day. Erin was taking a swim when she saw Caleb walking up to the beach house, where Carlyle was doing some reading. She noticed Ian standing a little ways off in the shade of a palm tree, impassive and watchful.

Erin knew Caleb's arrival meant either that the trouble was over, or that it had gotten worse. She swam back into the shallows, trying to quiet the sudden butterflies in her stomach. She came out onto the beach, grabbed the towel she'd left there, and wrapped it around her waist. She thought briefly of her pistol, just in case, but it was in the house next to the bed. That was fine. Ian had the situation covered.

She opened the door to find Carlyle and Caleb talking just inside. Carlyle looked past his security chief at her.

"All's well, darling," he said with a smile. "We're to be heading back home."

"When?" she asked, picking up another towel and starting to dry her hair.

"Just as soon as we can. We should be back in time for a late supper. Caleb's lad is at the airport, topping up the petrol for our flight."

"No further problems?" she asked.

"None," Caleb grunted. "Everything's taken care of."

"And Corky?" she asked Carlyle.

"He'll be away a bit longer," he replied. "There's a spot of business he's attending to south of the border, while he's out there. I'd not worry about him. He always turns up in the end. Go on outside, Caleb. We'll join you directly."

Caleb obediently stepped out. Erin went into the bedroom to change out of her swimsuit. Carlyle came with her.

"Can't a girl get some privacy?" she asked, smiling at him.

"If you want me to leave, you've only to ask," he said. "But I'd much rather have you where I can see you."

"I'll bet," she said, stripping off the suit. "Enjoy the show. We go back to work tomorrow."

It didn't take long to dress for the trip and pack their travel bags. Erin put on her usual New York outfit of slacks and button-down blouse, clipping the familiar burden of her.38 to her right ankle under her pants. Then they rejoined Caleb and Ian. Caleb had brought a Land Rover to take them to the airport. In less than an hour, with an astonishing lack of complications, they were airborne and headed north over the Caribbean.

Erin enjoyed the flight. It was certainly more comfortable than flying coach on a major airline. By the time they were off the Carolina coast, she was lightly buzzed. Carlyle had brought a couple of cases of excellent rum with them. He intended to add whatever was left to the Barley Corner's stock. Ian, considering himself on duty, stuck to bottled water.

"How far back do you and Caleb go?" she asked Carlyle.

"He's Evan's lad," Carlyle replied. "Not mine."

"Isn't that a little weird? Trusting your safety to somebody else's bodyguard?"

He shrugged. "I'd no choice in the matter. Evan's interests run through the Barley Corner. My name's on the deed, but that's largely a matter for the lawyers. Evan wanted one of his own men looking after security, just to make certain everything runs according to plan."

"You're Evans number-two guy," she protested. "He doesn't trust you to take care of his interests?"

"I've told you before, darling, trust isn't something Evan does. He doesn't trust me, nor anyone else. That's the Life, Erin."

She shivered. "I'm starting to understand why you fell for me. I'm not like that."

He laid a hand on her arm. "I know, darling, and that's one of the many reasons I love you."

"But you trust Ian," she said, nodding his direction. Ian was looking out the window and appeared not to be listening.

"That's different."

They landed at JFK just before seven. Erin hauled out her phone as they taxied in, dialing Michelle. Her brother would probably be at the hospital, working an ER shift.

"Hello?"

"Hey, Shelley, it's Erin. We just landed. How's Rolf doing?"

"Oh, he's been a real sport. You ought to get a couple of kids, Erin. He likes them, and Anna just adores him."

"Don't you start with me, Shelley. It's bad enough I have to deal with Mom. Thanks for taking him."

"It's no trouble, really. It's just... well... there is one thing."

"What's that?" Erin asked, more sharply than she intended.

"Anna put little pink bows in his hair. It may take a while to get them out."

Erin laughed. "Well, we'd better take care of that before work. I don't think the perps will respect him otherwise. I'll come by and pick him up. It'll be a little while yet. I don't have my car here at the airport."

"Okay, I'll see what I can do with his fur. See you soon."

"Bye, Shelley." Erin hung up, shaking her head.

"Ian and I can drop you at home," Carlyle offered. "It's not far from the Corner."

"Thanks," she said. "It'll be nice to get home and back to work. Is Caleb coming with us?"

"Nay, he's about some errands at the airport."

"Thanks," Erin called to Caleb as they got off the plane. "It was a good flight."

He grunted something unintelligible in acknowledgment.

* * *

Erin was pleased to note that this time she hadn't had the nightmares that had plagued her on her last trip out of town. Maybe she was getting to grips with the various critical incidents of the past year. Doc Evans, the Precinct 8 police psychologist, said she was handling things well and making good progress. Still, she knew that this city was where she really belonged. Riding north through Queens, her old stomping grounds, she let herself feel the pulse of the city. God, but she loved New York. Could you be a police officer in a city without loving it? She didn't ever want to find out.

"I can't leave here," she said to Carlyle. "Not permanently." They were riding in the back of his Mercedes. Ian was up front, driving with the same alertness he'd have had taking a convoy through Baghdad.

"I'd not ask you to," he said with a smile. "But thank you for coming away with me. I've been thinking."

"Do you ever stop?"

"Nay, it's something of a habit. In particular, I've been considering our situation. I think it may be time to bring your da into the picture."

"You sure about that?"

"Aye, he's bound to find out sooner or later. Better he hear it from you."

"Do you want to be there when I tell him?"

"That depends." Carlyle grinned. "Is he likely to be armed?"

"He likes to hunt," Erin reminded him. Her mom and dad had moved upstate after Sean's retirement. Sean O'Reilly had a very well-stocked gun case and plenty of ammunition.

"Then perhaps it's best you speak to him alone, before I go seeking his blessing."

"His blessing?" Erin echoed. Her heart skipped a beat. "Wait a second. Do you mean...?"

"Let's not run ahead of ourselves," Carlyle said. "All I'm saying now is that it might be best if your family knew about us."

"Let me think about it," she said. "It's going to take some planning. I better get Dad at the right time, in the right mood."

After that, as they crossed the East River into Manhattan, Erin found it difficult not to think about the future. But she wasn't as worried about it now. Maybe it was the vacation, maybe the lingering effects of that excellent Caribbean rum, but she thought everything just might be okay. Dad could be prickly, and he certainly didn't trust Carlyle, but Erin was his only daughter. She knew how to talk him around. She knew he was secretly tremendously proud she'd followed in his footsteps with the NYPD. There was a way to work things out. And then? She'd figure out how to deal with the police side of things after she'd sorted out her family.

Ian came to a stop right outside her apartment. Carlyle, ever the gentleman, offered to carry her luggage up.

"You do know I'm in better shape than you've ever been," she said with a smile.

"That's not precisely the point."

"I know. And I appreciate it. But I'm fine. I'll just run my bag up and then go get Rolf."

"Would you like me to wait on you?"

"No, that's okay. I'll be driving the Charger. I don't want to mess up your upholstery. I'll call you soon."

"I'll look forward to it. I love you, darling."

She kissed him lightly on the mouth. "You too. See you on the flip side."

Erin grabbed her suitcase and jogged up the stairs. She unlocked her apartment door and went inside, angling for the bedroom. She'd unpack later, but for now, she intended to bounce right back out and fetch Rolf. She missed her partner. The apartment felt terribly empty without the K-9. She tossed the suitcase onto her bed and turned back for the door.

"Evening, love."

Siobhan Finneran was standing next to the closet door. A Ruger .45 automatic was in her hand, pointed directly at Erin.

*   *   *

Erin's heart lurched. She thought of a dozen things to do, then discarded them all. Siobhan was an expert shot and a hardened killer. Rushing her would just get Erin gunned down. She couldn't possibly get to her ankle gun without tipping Siobhan off. Her other gun, the Glock, was in the closet behind Siobhan. Rolf was peacefully lounging around at her brother's house, pink ribbons in his fur. Erin's phone was in her pocket, and might as well be a thousand miles away.

"Evening," Erin said, pleasantly surprised at how calm she sounded. There was only a slight edge of tension in her voice. "Let yourself in, did you?"

Siobhan smiled. It was a fierce smile on that beautiful face, like the toothy grin of some great cat. "You weren't home, so I had to improvise."

"I think we need to talk," Erin said. She was careful to keep her hands out from her sides, in plain view.

"My thinking exactly," Siobhan said. "We've a few things to clear up between us."

"Whatever the problem is," Erin said, "I'll be glad to help you with it."

"Grand," Siobhan said. "But this could be a long conversation, and I don't imagine you do all your entertaining in your bedroom. Shall we step down the hall?"

"Sure." Erin thought of everything in her hallway and wished she had more furniture. There was nothing that could make any sort of distraction or improvised weapon.

"Slow and easy, love," Siobhan said, motioning with a slight movement of her pistol. "Turn around."

Erin turned her back on the other woman, though every instinct told her not to. Even murderers sometimes had trouble shooting someone while looking in their eyes. Executioners tended to blindfold their victims, or make them turn their backs.

The hairs on the back of her neck prickled as she walked slowly down the short hallway to her living room. Erin half-expected to feel the cold circle of the Ruger against the base of her skull, but Siobhan was too experienced for that. The hitwoman knew better than to get within arm's reach. Erin wouldn't be doing any fancy action-movie disarming trick.

"You don't have to do anything here," Erin said. "You can still walk away."

"Oh, I plan to," Siobhan said cheerfully. "Once we've concluded our business. And it's something I want to do. I've been looking forward to seeing you again."

"Have a seat," Erin offered, half turning to face Siobhan.

"Nay, love, I think I'll stand," Siobhan said. "But you can sit, if you please. Before you do, turn and spread your arms. Turn in a slow circle."

Erin did as she was told. Siobhan was looking for weapons, but didn't want to get close to pat her down. Erin felt a slight tingle of hope at that. If she could just get to the .38 at her ankle, she had a chance. She needed about two seconds to clear the holster and snap off a quick shot. But how to buy those two seconds remained a mystery.

"Now take out your phone. Slow and careful." The barrel of the Ruger traveled up until Erin was looking right down it. The hole was black and very large, like a subway tunnel with eternity waiting at the far end.

Erin obeyed. She held it out, thinking Siobhan would want it. But the other woman stayed where she was.

"You'll be making a telephone call," Siobhan said.

"To whom?"

"Your boyfriend, of course. And you'll say just what I tell you."

"And what's that?"

"You'll tell him you forgot something, a little present you got him from your time in the Caribbean. You'll ask him to come over and step up to your flat."

"So you can shoot him? Screw you, Finneran. I'll do no such thing."

Siobhan's smile didn't falter. "You think I want to shoot him? That's not what this is about, love. This is about clearing up our little misunderstandings."

"What if he won't come? He's got things to take care of."

"Convince him. Sure but you're the persuasive one. And don't you drop a hint of anything out of the ordinary. You'll be putting him on speaker, obviously, and I'll be listening. You say one thing wrong and I'll shoot you low down, so you bleed out screaming. You think he'll like listening to that? I'm guessing that would bring him running in a hurry."

Erin looked for a way out. She couldn't see one, not yet. Maybe, just maybe Carlyle was persuasive enough. Maybe he'd be able to do something with this woman who Erin was now sure was completely out of her mind. And she had one card she could play.

"Okay," she said. "I'm calling now." She redialed the number of Carlyle's current burner phone and pushed the speaker button, just as Siobhan had told her. The phone rang once. Twice.

"Careful," Siobhan reminded her, wiggling the barrel of her pistol meaningfully.

On the third ring, Carlyle answered. "Evening, darling," he said. He sounded calm and happy. "Miss me already?"

Erin had already decided what to say. "You know I do, sweetheart," she said, keeping her own tone light, trying her best not to give the word any undue emphasis, nothing to tip Siobhan off. "That's why I'm calling. There's something I forgot to give you, from our trip. A little surprise."

"That's intriguing," he said. "Are you wanting to bring it over, or shall I come fetch it?"

"Why don't you come back to my place?"

Siobhan nodded approvingly. There was no hint of suspicion in the Irishwoman's cold green eyes.

"Grand," Carlyle said. "I can be there in a few minutes. Shall I come up?"

"Yeah. The door's unlocked."

"Shouldn't do that, sweetheart," Carlyle said. "Not in this town. I'll be there directly."

Siobhan signaled to Erin to hang up. She did.

"Grand work," Siobhan said with a mocking smile. "Now sit down. On the couch. Be sure to leave room for your lover. He'll be joining us shortly."

Erin sat. Carlyle had echoed their code word back to her. He'd heard it. What would he do? She had no choice but to wait, and to trust him.

The next five minutes were five of the longest of Erin O'Reilly's life.

Chapter 15

The click of the latch on the apartment's front door sounded as sharp as a gunshot to Erin. Siobhan stepped smoothly to the end of the couch so she was covering both Erin and the entryway.

The door swung open. Carlyle walked in. He didn't look any different than usual. His face was absolutely unreadable. He took in the two women at a glance.

"Siobhan, darling," he said, completely ignoring the gun in her hand. "This is unexpected. I didn't know Erin had a visitor. I hope I'm not intruding."

"Evening, Cars," Siobhan said. "Do come in and join us."

Carlyle stepped into the living room, leaving the door to swing shut on its own. "Would you be wanting something to drink?" he asked. "Perhaps Erin's already offered."

"Not just now," Siobhan said. "Come here. Now."

"As you please," Carlyle said. He made the briefest eye contact with Erin, but she didn't know what he was planning. All she'd managed to communicate to him was that she was in trouble, that she was being coerced into the telephone call. For all he'd known, there might have been a room full of armed

Mafia goons waiting for him. Had he really just decided to walk in alone and unarmed? Where was Ian?

"Not carrying, are you?" Siobhan asked him, reading Erin's mind.

"You know I don't carry a piece," Carlyle said. "I've not turned into such an American as that."

Siobhan smiled at that. "Grand. I'll take you at your word. Would you care to sit?"

"If you're standing, I'll do the same," Carlyle said, returning her smile. He walked into the living room and moved toward the television, opposite the couch where Erin sat.

"Get over there with your slag," Siobhan snapped, the smile dropping suddenly off her face.

Carlyle's eyes went cold and hard. "I'll not have you using words like that around me, lass," he said.

Words like what? Erin wanted to ask. She didn't know that particular Irish slang term, though she could guess at the meaning, judging from the context and Carlyle's reaction. But that wasn't really the point. The point was that Carlyle and Siobhan were feeling each other out, testing boundaries. If this was a fight, it had already started. She just needed Siobhan to look away for two seconds. Whatever happened, she had to be ready to grab that chance. It might be the only one she'd get. Even if Siobhan got her, she had to take the woman down.

"You're a truth-telling man, Cars," Siobhan said, with a slight pout. "You raised me to be telling the truth. I'm just calling her what she is."

"She's as much a part of my life as yourself, Siobhan," Carlyle said. "I'm not asking you to love her, but I'm asking you to accept her. I know I'm important to you. Erin's important to me. Can you respect that?"

"She's never accepted me," Siobhan spat back. "The manky bitch threw me in jail. Twice!"

"She was only doing her job."

"My da was killed by men like her, doing their job!" she shouted. "Don't tell me you've forgotten!"

"I've forgotten none of it," Carlyle said. "And she'd nothing to do with the Troubles, darling. What's made you so angry at her?"

"She's a feckin' thief!"

"I don't understand. What is it she's stolen?"

"You!"

Carlyle's face froze, and Erin saw him finally get it. She'd tried to tell him, gently, in their previous talks about Siobhan. When he looked at her, he saw his friend's daughter, a sweet little girl who'd needed a father in her life. He'd tried, along with Corky and some of the others from his IRA unit, to fill that gap. But Siobhan had grown up. She'd probably grown up way too fast, in turbulent and violent times, and she was a woman now. She didn't look at Carlyle as a father.

"Oh, darling," he said quietly, with a softness in his face completely at odds with the pistol that was still pointed at him and Erin. "I love you, Siobhan. You know that. You'll not lose that, not to anyone, never."

"You stand here and say that?" Siobhan demanded. "To my bloody face? You had a choice, and you chose her! You sold me out to the bloody coppers, so don't you dare lie to me!"

"I'm telling the truth, darling. And I was trying to help the both of you. Why do you think I showed you that back door to the Corner?"

Erin knew Carlyle hadn't shown Siobhan the emergency exit that had let her slip away from the ESU tactical team with any intention of her using it that night, but that wasn't the point. The point was to convince Siobhan to put away the gun. Or, barring that, to buy Erin the two seconds she needed. Maybe

Carlyle would forgive her if she put Siobhan down with a bullet, maybe he wouldn't, but she'd have to take that chance.

"You chose her," Siobhan said again, and there were tears shining in her eyes. "How could you?"

"This was never about choosing sides," Carlyle said. He took a step toward her, his hands open, like he meant to embrace her.

"It's always about choosing sides!" Siobhan retorted. "That's all anyone ever does. If the Troubles taught me nothing else, they taught me that!"

"And look where that got Ireland," he said. "We only started healing when we stopped fighting. You keep picking at the wound, Siobhan, and it never stops bleeding."

"They murdered my da! They murdered your wife, for God's sake! What the hell do you know about bleeding? You've nothing but ice in you if you're willing to walk away from that!"

"But that's what I had to do, darling." Erin had never seen Carlyle more persuasive. He'd told her he'd walked into meetings with men who'd intended to kill him and talked them out of it, and now she believed it. He was trying to meet Siobhan's anger and absorb it.

"I had to walk away," he continued. "Because it was tearing me up from the inside. I know where the hate comes from, darling, and I still feel it. I'd want to kill the bastards who murdered my Rosie, aye. But it'd not bring her back to me."

"I got one of them for you," Siobhan said defiantly. "And it felt good, whatever you say. And I told him, right before I blew out his God damned brains, 'This is for Rosie McCann.' I saw in his eyes, he knew. He was guilty as Satan himself. And then I snuffed him, the bloody gobshite, and let him take that thought with him right down to Hell. Stand back!"

The last two words came out like the crack of a whip. Carlyle stopped. He'd almost gotten within arm's reach of her.

Maybe he'd been intending to try to disarm her and maybe not, but Siobhan was taking no chances. Carlyle stopped.

"Or what, darling? You're going to shoot me?"

"If you make me."

"No one's making you do anything, lass," he said. "Whatever happens in this room, it's in your hands and on your soul." Holding his hands up in a placating gesture, he stepped back and around Siobhan, backing toward the living room window.

Siobhan tracked him with the pistol, her face an incomprehensible mix of anger, sadness, betrayal, love, and hate.

"What is it you want, darling?" Carlyle asked. "Why did you come here?"

"I came for you," Siobhan said. "To save you."

"From what?"

"From her." Siobhan angrily twitched the barrel of the Ruger toward Erin, who felt an involuntary tightness in her gut as the muzzle swept across in front of her face. "She's making you into something you're not."

"What am I, Siobhan?" he asked gently.

"You're Cars Carlyle!" she said. "You're the one the other lads come to, the one they trust. You know how to get what everyone wants. You're the one man I could always trust. And you hurt me. You gave me to her!"

"That's not what happened, darling," Carlyle said. "I was trying to protect you."

"She told you that!" Siobhan spat. "She's in your head. I never thought a floozy would be calling the shots for you. I thought you were strong! I looked up to you! You're all I ever wanted. What's she got that I don't? Tell me that!"

"Darling, I love the both of you," Carlyle said. "It's different. You're a daughter to me."

"I'm not your bloody daughter! Just because you lost your baby when Rose got killed doesn't mean you get to turn me into the kid you couldn't have!"

In spite of his self-control, Carlyle flinched as if she'd slapped him. He recovered almost immediately, but Erin saw the pain in his eyes. She wondered if she should say something, but she knew she'd likely only make things worse. She kept watching, waiting for her chance.

"I know you've always been your own person, darling," Carlyle said. "And I've no wish to turn you into something you're not. But I can't give you what you're asking."

"Because of her?"

"Nay. Because I do think of you as my daughter, and that's how I love you, how I'll always love you. That's what you need to understand. Just because I love someone else, too, doesn't mean—"

It was a mistake. Erin saw it, and saw the realization of it on Carlyle's face. The thought of sharing him with anyone else was the one thing Siobhan just couldn't stand. She wanted everything, what Erin's dad would've called the whole Popsicle stand.

"I saved her life," Siobhan said with quiet venom dripping from every word. "For you. I should have let her burn."

"I'd never have forgiven you," Carlyle said softly, still trying to salvage the situation.

"I don't need your forgiveness," Siobhan said. Her face had gone very pale. Her jaw was tight. "Have you done anything that needs forgiving?"

"Any number of things," Carlyle said.

Erin tensed. She saw Siobhan making up her mind. Out of the corner of her eye, she saw movement in the entryway and wondered what it was.

"Then maybe I need to do something you can forgive," Siobhan said softly. "Then we can forgive one another."

"That's not how this works," Carlyle said.

"I don't know about that," Siobhan said. "But I do know how some things work. I know how guns work, and bullets, and killing. You lads in the Brigades made certain of that. And I was a grand learner. Let me show you what I know."

Abruptly, the Irishwoman turned to Erin. The Ruger came up and Erin was staring down the barrel once more. She saw the finger starting to tighten on the trigger. It was almost too quick for her to feel afraid. The only thought in her mind was, *No. Not yet.* But Erin O'Reilly had run out of time.

Carlyle lunged toward Siobhan, his hand reaching for her gun.

Siobhan spun, quick as a cat, startled but vicious. She fired. The roar of the Ruger was enormous, echoing off the walls of the small room.

Carlyle stumbled, doubled over, and started to fall. His hands went to his stomach.

Erin was screaming in her head, but her body was moving. Her right hand dropped to her ankle, snatching at the grip of her snub-nosed .38. Siobhan was standing frozen, staring at the man she loved, in her own sick way, more than anyone else on Earth.

The .38 was in Erin's hand, coming up, but Siobhan's eye had caught the motion and she was turning, her face now showing just one emotion: absolute, murderous fury. In slow motion, Erin watched the pistol swinging toward her as she willed her hand to move faster.

There was another gunshot, a flat, hard crack. Both women started, but neither had fired. The shot came from behind Siobhan, from the entryway. Siobhan twisted sharply, as if struck a hard blow in the back. But she stayed on her feet and still tried to bring her gun to bear on Erin.

That half-second of hesitation was what Erin had needed. She fired the revolver at a range of less than five feet. The bullet punched into Siobhan's belly, right under the rib cage. Siobhan's legs buckled. The .45 fell from her hand as she went down.

Erin jumped to her feet, keeping her gun trained on the fallen woman. Ian Thompson came into the room. His Beretta was in his hand, smoke curling from the muzzle.

Ian had been Carlyle's backup plan. He must have come into the room low, keeping out of sight, after Carlyle had entered. He'd been waiting. Why couldn't he have done something sooner? There was no time to worry about that. Erin kicked the Ruger away from Siobhan. The assassin was still alive, watching her, but Erin could see the eyes starting to lose their focus. She'd taken Ian's bullet close to the spine, probably puncturing a lung, and Erin's shot had gone through the diaphragm. Either wound was lethal.

"Cover her," Erin ordered Ian as she snatched out her phone and speed-dialed 911. She bent over Carlyle. He was doubled up on the carpet, a shocking pool of dark red spreading out from him, soaking into the light gray rug.

"911 emergency. Please state the nature of your emergency," Dispatch answered.

"This is Detective O'Reilly," she said, dropping to her knees on the floor. "Shield four-six-four-oh. I need a bus, forthwith. Two GSW victims, one abdominal wound, one with two in the torso."

"What's your address, O'Reilly?"

Erin rattled off her apartment information as she examined Carlyle. He'd been hit in the gut, never a good place to take a bullet. His face had gone an awful grayish color from near-instantaneous shock. He was only semi-conscious. She thought maybe he was in too much pain even to be able to scream. Blood pumped between his fingers. So much of it. It was everywhere.

"*Bus is en route,*" Dispatch reported. "*First responders have been notified. Patrol units should arrive momentarily.*"

Erin dropped the phone without bothering to hang up. "Look at me," she told Carlyle. "Talk to me. Come on!"

His eyes tried to focus on her. His jaw was clenched tightly. He managed a slight nod.

"I need to see the wound," she said. Then, realizing Siobhan wasn't an immediate problem, she glanced at Ian. "Towels from the bathroom!"

Ian nodded and sprinted down the hall. He came back with an armful of towels.

Carlyle made his hands uncurl. Even more blood pulsed out. Erin couldn't see the wound. There was too much blood. Ian was at her side now, handing her a folded towel.

"Pressure on the abdomen," she told him.

"I know," he said softly, and Erin remembered he'd probably been around at least as many wounded men as she had.

"The ambulance is on the way," she told Carlyle, putting a hand behind his head. "Talk to me. Stay conscious. You're going to be fine."

"It's... all right... darling," he whispered.

"Yeah," she said. "Everything's okay. We're going to take care of you."

"Doesn't... hurt so much... now. Just cold."

Erin fought down the panic she felt trying to climb out of her throat. She remembered Brunanski, the police officer in Queens. She'd held him in her arms, shot the same way, and he'd died. "Not you," she said grimly. "Not now. You don't get to die on me, Carlyle. Don't you dare."

"Maybe... it's better... like this," he said. "We always... knew... this would be... how it..."

"No!" She almost shouted the denial at him. Her other hand found his, gripping it tightly, as if she could hold life in him by squeezing his fingers. His blood was hot and sticky. "This isn't the end. Not yet."

"Liver, I think," Ian muttered beside her. "No exit wound. Bullet's still in there." He was holding the towel, which had turned deep crimson.

"What kept you?" Erin asked him.

"Sorry, ma'am. Mr. Carlyle told me not to start shooting unless someone was getting killed. Then I didn't have a clean shot. Might've hit you with the overpenetration."

"You should've taken the shot anyway," Erin said and instantly regretted it. "Sorry. This wasn't your fault. Thanks for the help." Where was that goddamn ambulance? She could hear sirens, but they still sounded far away, echoing like they were coming through the Lincoln Tunnel.

"Ian... lad?" Carlyle whispered.

"Yes, sir. I'm here."

"Erin... wanted to know... about your tattoos."

Erin and Ian glanced at each other, sharing the same thought that this was an unusual time for that question.

"Added one for each confirmed shot," Ian said. "One per kill."

"Why?" Erin asked.

"Don't know. Superstition, maybe. Got to be a habit."

"I've never shot a woman before," Erin said, glancing at Siobhan. The other woman's eyes were open, staring glassily at the ceiling. If she was still breathing, Erin couldn't see it.

"I have," Ian said quietly.

"I've... never shot... anyone," Carlyle managed.

"That's not true," Erin said. "You winged that German guy at the Corner last year."

Carlyle smiled very shakily. "He... didn't die." Then he stopped smiling. "Hail... Mary. Full of... grace. The Lord... is with thee. Blessed... art thou... among... women..."

"No," Erin said. "No." Like any good Catholic, she knew the Hail Mary by heart. And she knew what it meant when an injured man started saying it.

"NYPD!" someone shouted. The sound still had that echoing quality. Erin realized she was in shock herself. That could play tricks on your hearing. She looked up and saw a pair of uniformed officers in the doorway, guns in their hands. They took in the scene at once, going to Siobhan to start first aid on her.

"Where's the damn bus?" Erin asked them.

"Saw it coming down the street," one of the cops said. "Just a few seconds behind us. You O'Reilly?"

"Yeah," she said, trying to place the face. She'd seen him around the precinct but couldn't remember his name.

"Who's this guy?" the cop asked, indicating Ian.

"Bystander," she said.

"In your apartment?" the cop wondered aloud. Then he shrugged. "Barty, what've you got there?"

"She's gone, Sarge," the other cop said. "I think her heart got clipped. Nothing I can do."

Two paramedics came in the door. They'd been delayed getting their stretcher up the elevator. They approached the two bodies on the ground. The uniformed officer next to Siobhan shook his head at them.

"We've got this now," one of the EMTs told Erin. "We'll take over."

"Single GSW, abdomen," she told them. "We better get him to Bellevue. They've got a good trauma ward and—"

"We've got this," the EMT said again, and this time he got through to her. Erin sat back, but she didn't let go of Carlyle's hand while the medics went to work.

"Be with... us sinners..." Carlyle said, slurring his words in a way she'd never heard him do, no matter how much he'd had to drink.

"No way, Carlyle," she told him. "Not on my watch."

"We've gotta get him out of here," one EMT said to the other. "Now. We're losing him."

Chapter 16

"Hang on," Erin told Carlyle. The ambulance's siren howled, punctuated by blasts from the horn. She hadn't let go of his hand, which felt cold against her palm. She was hunched against the wall of the vehicle, trying to stay out of the EMT's way.

The medic had a saline bag pumping fluid back in, trying to keep Carlyle's blood pressure up. He'd put a pre-warmed blanket over Carlyle's legs to try to keep his body temperature good. He was keeping direct pressure on the wound.

She could hear the driver on his radio, talking to the hospital. "Got a single GSW coming in, white male, age fifty. Abdominal wound, no exit, large caliber handgun. Heavy bleeding, severe hypotension, potential liver damage. Severe shock. He's gonna need a doc, stat."

"We're almost there," Erin said, hoping it was true. She couldn't see the street from where she was sitting, so had no idea where in Manhattan they were. "Don't you give up now. I've got you."

"Sorry..." Carlyle mumbled.

"You've got nothing to be sorry for," she said. She felt tears filling her eyes and angrily blinked them back. If she could keep from crying, some superstitious part of her brain whispered, maybe he wouldn't die.

"Coming up on the ER," the driver called back.

The ambulance swung around a curve and slowed to a halt. Almost before it had stopped moving, the back doors were open and a team from the Bellevue ER was there, hoisting the stretcher out. Erin got out alongside, refusing to let go. They hurried through the doors of the emergency room. A doctor was there, asking questions, looking at Carlyle.

"Okay, let's get him into OR two, stat," he said. "Get two units of type O, cross and type him for three more." He paused. "Jesus Christ, Erin?"

Erin blinked and stared blankly at him. It took her a second to recognize her brother.

"Are you hurt?" Sean asked as the orderlies wheeled them toward the operating room. "Christ, you've got blood all over you."

She shook her head numbly.

"Okay, sis," he said. "I've got this. Who is this guy? What's his name?"

"I can't tell you right now."

"Okay," Sean said again. "Erin, he needs surgery right now. You need to stay out here. I'm going to scrub in."

"Sean?"

"Yeah?" He was all business now, a trauma surgeon having just another evening in the ER.

"Save him."

His flash of irritation cut through the fog in her brain. "That's my job, kiddo. It's what I do." Then his eyes softened for a moment. "Who is this guy?" he asked her again, more quietly.

Erin licked her lips. "He's mine," she managed to say.

Sean put out a hand and grasped her shoulder, just for a second. Then she found herself outside the doors to the operating rooms, all by herself. She stood there, suddenly unable to move. She started shaking all over.

"Ma'am? Do you need a doctor?"

A nurse was at Erin's elbow, looking at her with professional concern.

"No," she said, clutching her elbows. "No, I'm fine."

"Doctor O'Reilly will take good care of him," the nurse said, nodding toward the OR. "He's one of the best."

"He's my brother."

"Then your brother's in good hands."

"No," Erin said. "Doctor O'Reilly is my brother."

"Oh." The nurse was momentarily perplexed. "Well, maybe you'd like to get cleaned up a little. It will probably be a while."

Erin made herself walk to the restroom. The face that met her in the mirror shocked her. She was sheet white, her eyes hollow and haunted. Blood was all over her. Not just on her hands and arms, but spattered across her chest and cheeks. The knees of her slacks were soaked where she'd knelt on her carpet. She looked like a zombie in some cheap horror movie.

"God," she whispered. She started the warm water running in the sink and almost fell over. She was ashamed of her weakness. Sean O'Reilly's daughter should be tougher than that. She could handle this. She gripped the sides of the sink, leaving bloody fingerprints, and clenched her hands until her arms trembled. She forced herself to look into her own eyes.

"You can do this," she said through gritted teeth. She remembered something Ian had told her a while ago. "Dig deep, find more, keep going."

She did what she could with hot water and paper towels, which wasn't much. Then she went back to the waiting area and tumbled into a vacant chair. She wanted to just switch off, to feel nothing for hours, maybe forever.

That wasn't an option. She needed to call Webb. She reached for her phone.

It wasn't in her pocket.

"Damn it," Erin muttered. She'd left it at her apartment, which was now an active crime scene. Hell, the phone was probably in an evidence bag by now. There was a phone in the room, but a half-hysterical woman was using it, dealing with her own personal crisis.

So Erin tried to settle in to wait. Sean would come out when the operation was over, whatever had happened. Either Carlyle would pull through, or he wouldn't. Either way, she'd done all she could for him short of praying. And so she prayed.

*   *   *

Erin didn't rate an angel from Heaven. What she got instead was a grumpy Russian and a worn-out gumshoe from LA. Vic and Webb found her in the waiting room half an hour later. Neither one of them looked good. Erin supposed they'd been called away from home after a long workday.

"Are you okay?" Vic asked, looking her over. "Damn, you got blood head to foot."

She nodded wearily. "I'm fine."

"Welcome back to New York," Webb said sourly. "You decided to announce your return by blowing away a home invader and then leaving the scene?"

"How'd you hear about it?" she asked, ignoring the question.

"Caught it on the police band on my car radio," Vic said. "On my way home from the liquor store. They said there'd been an officer-involved shooting. They didn't give your name, but I helped you move in last year, remember? I recognized the address. Just about drove my car into a lamppost when I heard it. Who'd you shoot?"

"Siobhan Finneran," Erin said.

"Say what now?" Vic said.

"We heard you," Webb said. "What was she doing in your apartment?"

"Trying to kill me."

"Okay," Webb said. "We've got her dead at the scene, one guy in custody, another one in the hospital here. Who are they?"

There was absolutely no point in lying or misleading them. They'd know the truth soon enough. Erin took a deep breath. "Ian Thompson's the guy they held at the scene. Morton... Morton Carlyle's in surgery right now."

Vic whistled softly. "Carlyle finally decided to get his hands dirty, huh? And you shot him?"

Erin shook her head. "Siobhan shot him."

"And you shot Siobhan?" Vic asked.

"Thompson and I did, yeah," Erin said. "Is he under arrest?"

"If he's not, he's going to be," Webb said.

"He was protecting me," Erin said.

Webb shook his head. "That doesn't matter, O'Reilly. You just told me he shot a woman. Until we sort this out, he's under arrest. Obviously."

"Erin," Vic said. "If Siobhan came to your apartment to kill you, and ended up shooting Carlyle, what the hell was Carlyle doing there? Did she shoot him by accident?"

Erin didn't say anything. She didn't know what to say. She was too tired, too scared to dissemble.

"O'Reilly," Webb said quietly. "This is now a major case. We're going to have to treat it that way. I don't think I want to know, but I need to know. Where have you been the past week?"

Erin looked at the two of them, men she'd come to trust and consider her friends. Nothing was left but the truth.

"I was in the Bahamas," she said quietly. "With Carlyle."

Webb's face was like granite. "Anyone else with you?"

"Ian Thompson."

"Why were you there?"

"Carlyle asked me to go with him."

"What was he doing there?"

"Nothing. Nothing illegal, I mean. He was taking a few days out of town because of the attempted shooting last week."

"What is the nature of your relationship with Morton Carlyle?"

"Why are you asking me that, sir?"

"Because Internal Affairs is going to ask you the same thing," Webb said. "And that's not the only thing they're going to ask."

"Erin, what the hell?" Vic demanded.

"Keep out of this, Neshenko," Webb snapped.

Vic didn't even seem to hear Webb. The look in his eyes went beyond betrayal. He was staring at Erin as if she was a complete stranger. "Erin, what the fuck did you do?"

"God damn it, Neshenko, that's enough!" Webb shouted.

The emergency room became instantly silent around them. All three detectives were reminded where they were. No one had been listening to them until now. Two nurses, a couple of orderlies, the duty nurse behind the desk, and half a dozen patients and family members were staring at them with wide eyes.

Vic's face twisted. "I don't believe this shit," he said.

"Vic," Erin began, but didn't know how to finish.

"Neshenko, you're going to drive us back to the Eight," Webb said, his voice quivering on the edge of control. "O'Reilly, do you have your car here?"

"No, sir. I rode in the ambulance."

"Then you're riding with us. Neshenko, you're not going to say one word. Not one."

"I need to stay here, sir," Erin said. "I have to be here when—"

"No," Webb interrupted coldly. "You need to come with me, right now. Until I know exactly what happened tonight, you're going to be where I can keep an eye on you."

Erin set her jaw. "I'm staying here, sir."

"You're coming with us, or I'm arresting you as an accessory," Webb snapped.

It was Erin's turn to stare at her commanding officer as if she'd never seen him before. "You mean that?"

"Get. In. The. Car." Each word was its own sentence.

Erin almost said no. But she was still a cop, for one more night at least. So she followed her commander's orders and went with him into the parking lot. Vic, furious but smart enough to keep silent, stalked on the other side of Webb. He didn't look at Erin.

*   *   *

According to the clock, it was after nine when the detectives got to the precinct. Erin mechanically obeyed Webb's instructions that she sit down in the Major Crimes break room and not talk to anyone. He asked for her phone, so she told him she'd left it on the floor at the apartment. Webb made a couple of calls. Vic sat at his desk and glared at nothing in particular until Webb put him to work talking to the CSU guys who were, at that moment, going through Erin's living room.

Erin waited. It occurred to her that she'd be doing exactly the same thing if she'd stayed at the hospital, but that didn't make her feel any better. She should be there. What if Carlyle came out of surgery? What if he asked for her? What if he died on the table? Sean would try to call her as soon as he was done operating, but she didn't have her damn phone. She cursed herself for fifteen different kinds of idiot for leaving it behind.

Captain Holliday came into the office. Erin watched him through the window in the break-room door. He was an old-school cop in his mid-fifties with a mustache that reminded Erin of the marshals in old Westerns. He had a reputation as a patient, fair-minded guy, a good commander. Now, pulled away from home in the middle of what should've been a quiet evening, he still looked outwardly calm, but Erin saw the concern in his face as he exchanged a few words with Webb. Then he went into his office and closed the door.

After a few more minutes, the man arrived that Erin most expected and least wanted to see. Lieutenant Andrew Keane, the Bloodhound, Precinct 8's head of Internal Affairs. If he'd been interrupted doing something else, he gave no sign of it. His suit was as neatly pressed as ever, his shoes shined to a reflective finish, his cheeks smooth-shaven. His eyes were sharp and alert. He shook Webb's hand once, briskly, and also disappeared into Captain Holliday's office.

Webb walked over to the break room and opened the door. "Okay, O'Reilly," he said. "You and me. Captain's office."

Wordlessly, Erin followed him. Webb closed the door behind them. Holliday's office was comfortable, but it wasn't big, and there were only three chairs, counting the Captain's own leather swivel behind his desk. It was a little crowded. Holliday was seated there, grim-faced, hands clasped on top of his desk. Keane was standing next to the window, arms at his sides. When he met Erin's eyes, one corner of his mouth quirked up in a sardonic hint of a smile. It wasn't a comforting expression.

"Lieutenant, Detective, take a seat," Holliday said, nodding to the two empty chairs. Erin sat, trying to keep her back straight, and made herself look the Captain in the face. Webb sank heavily into the other chair with a slight sigh. His fingers twitched, and Erin knew Webb was wishing he had a cigarette. At that moment, she wouldn't have minded one herself. Anything to take her mind off what was happening. It felt like a nightmare she couldn't wake from.

"Lieutenant Webb has told me a little of what's happened," Holliday said. "I understand we have a serious situation. Detective O'Reilly, do you want a lawyer from the Union to be present?"

Erin started at the suggestion. She hadn't even thought about it. "No, sir," she said, squaring her shoulders.

"Lieutenant Keane, for the record, Detective O'Reilly has waived legal representation for this meeting," Holliday said. "Now, Detective, I'm aware there has been a fatal shooting at your residence this evening, and that you were the officer involved. Is that correct?"

"Yes, sir."

"Obviously, we will be requiring the usual paperwork. This isn't your first shooting incident, so I assume you know the general framework of what's required?"

"Yes, sir." Those were definitely the safest words for her to use. Erin intended to repeat them as often as possible.

"Please tell us how this happened," Holliday said. "From the beginning."

"From the beginning," Erin repeated. How was she going to explain this? "It started last year on my first day with Major Crimes," she began.

"Maybe not quite that far back?" Holliday prompted gently.

"This is relevant, sir. We were investigating a car bombing. One of the suspects was a member of the O'Malley organization, Morton Carlyle. In the course of the investigation, I was at his bar, the Barley Corner, when a bomb was delivered. With Carlyle's help, Skip Taylor from the Bomb Squad and I were able to disarm the device. Carlyle considered this a favor, since I'd saved his life and his place of business. Over the following months, we communicated on matters pertinent to my cases. His information proved valuable on several occasions."

"Carlyle was your CI in the O'Malleys?" Webb asked.

"That's correct, sir," Erin said.

"You were aware of the existence of an informant, Lieutenant, but not of his identity?" Keane asked Webb.

"That's right," Webb said.

"Detective O'Reilly," Keane said. "Is Mr. Carlyle's identity as an informant known to any other law enforcement officer outside this room?"

"No, sir."

"Is his status as a CI documented anywhere?"

"No, sir."

"Why not?"

Erin faced Keane. "It wasn't necessary for any investigation up to now. We never needed his testimony in court, and he would have refused to testify in any case."

"So all we have is your word that he has cooperated with the NYPD?" Keane asked.

Erin bristled. "I'm not lying. Sir."

Holliday raised a hand. "Lieutenant Keane, please. Let's avoid leveling any accusations."

"You misunderstand me, Captain," Keane said. "I'm not accusing Detective O'Reilly of anything. I'm simply attempting to determine the underpinnings of the situation. Please, Detective, continue."

"Over time, Carlyle and I became more closely acquainted," Erin said. "He was always reliable, and as helpful as he could be while operating under his constraints."

"What constraints were those?" Holliday asked.

"He refused to give information pertaining directly to the O'Malleys and their associates," she said. "The Irish have a tradition against informants and traitors. There would have been a strong stigma attached to his actions if they became known. And one of the O'Malleys probably would have killed him. His association with me was known to the O'Malley leadership, so if he'd given me something that was used against them, he would've been compromised."

"Is your relationship with Mr. Carlyle emotionally intimate?" Keane asked.

Being embarrassed about it wouldn't help. Erin looked Keane straight in the eye as she answered.

"Yes, sir."

"Physically intimate, as well?"

"Yes, sir."

"Detective O'Reilly," Holliday said. "You are not a case agent, you have no authority to review CI status. You realize how this relationship compromises you? How it could compromise prior cases? This could jeopardize convictions in cases in which you have participated, if you are found to have engaged in professional misconduct."

"It hasn't compromised anything I've done," she said, aware she sounded petulant and defensive. "We've caught guys we wouldn't have caught without him. He's the reason we stopped that guy from blowing up One PP last year. Hundreds of people would be dead if not for him."

"The ends don't automatically justify the means," Holliday said. "That's not how we work. That's not who we are. What gifts has he given you?"

"Gifts?" Erin echoed. "Nothing big. I mean, he put me up at a place in the Hamptons for a week. And he flew me to the Bahamas last week. So, a couple of trips. And a few bottles of whiskey. Some dinners. The sort of thing a guy does when he's dating someone."

"What have you done for the O'Malleys?" Keane asked. "I can only assume if, as you say, they know about you, that they expected something from you?"

"I've arrested O'Malleys," Erin said sharply. "More than once. I haven't shielded them."

"I didn't say you had," Keane said. "I asked what you did at their request."

"I got a tipoff about a drug shipment," she said. "One belonging to the Lucarellis. Over a million in heroin. I've taken action on some other information. I think they see my value primarily as a way of hurting their competition. But everyone I've busted has been a criminal, engaged in committing a major felony. They were clean busts."

"Have you taken any money from Mr. Carlyle?" Keane asked.

"Not a cent." As she said it, Erin realized Carlyle had always avoided giving or offering her any money. That was probably because of this very situation. He hadn't wanted her to be in the position of taking cash from him, no matter the reason. He'd staked her in a card game once, but she hadn't kept any of the cash. He'd been trying to protect her from the start. She remembered how he'd thrown himself on top of her when she'd called out a warning about the bomb at the Corner. Even before he'd been her lover, he'd been prepared to shield her. Tears prickled the corners of her eyes. No, not now, she inwardly begged. She couldn't lose it now. Not in front of these men.

"This Finneran woman who was shot this evening," Holliday said. "How does she fit into this?"

"She's an Irishwoman who lost her father during the Troubles, when she was a little girl," Erin explained. "Her dad was in the IRA and was an associate of Carlyle's. He stepped in and helped raise her. He considered it a foster-parent situation, but over time, she developed an obsessive attachment to him. She thought I was a romantic rival and tried to kill me so she could have him to herself."

"So she was completely unrelated to the O'Malley situation?" Holliday asked.

"Not exactly, sir. She was an assassin who killed several people for them. That includes three men that she shot behind that restaurant in Little Italy earlier this year, along with planting the bomb that killed Hans Rüdel near One PP. That's four we know of for sure. There may have been others."

"But she shot Carlyle," Webb said.

"Carlyle saw Siobhan was about to shoot me," Erin said. "He jumped in the way. Then his driver and I shot her, before she could kill me, too."

"Who's the driver?" Holliday asked.

"Ian Thompson," Webb said. "We've got him downstairs, in lockup."

Holliday rubbed his mustache. "This has the makings of an absolute disaster," he said softly.

"I disagree, Captain," Keane said.

Every head in the room turned toward him in surprise.

"I see it as an opportunity," he continued.

"I think you'd better explain, Lieutenant," Holliday said.

"Certainly," Keane said. "But before I do, I'd like to commend Detective O'Reilly's discretionary impulse. I believe she was completely correct to keep this association as quiet as possible. That is why the opportunity exists in the first place, and if we are to fully exploit it, that habit of secrecy will need to be continued. Therefore, Captain, I think you and I should discuss this between ourselves."

Holliday nodded slowly. "All right. Lieutenant Webb, Detective O'Reilly, please step outside. Not a word to anyone.

And don't leave the building. I'll want to talk to you again shortly. Please close the door behind you."

Webb and Erin dutifully got up, saluted, and left. Webb closed the door to Holliday's office.

"What's going on, sir?" Erin dared to ask.

"I have no idea," Webb said. "I might be in a better position to answer that question if I'd had more information going in."

Erin winced. "Yes, sir."

"It looks like we've got a little time here," Webb said. "So I'd like you to start on your incident report. You've got a fair amount of paperwork to take care of. Where's the gun you used?"

"I left it at my apartment," she said. "On the floor. It's a snub-nosed .38 revolver. Fired once."

"Then the CSU guys will have it," Webb said. "Good. Sit down and get to work."

Erin started to sit, then paused. "Sir?"

"Now what, O'Reilly?" Webb asked wearily.

"Where's Vic?"

Webb looked at Vic's empty chair. He used several words he'd probably picked up on the streets of LA, in a combination Erin had never heard before. He ended with, "And I swear, if that goddamned mother-loving son of a cornholing Brighton Beach florist is screwing up something else, I am personally going to ram my boot so far up his ass I'll have to reach up his nose to tie my laces."

By the time he'd finished, Erin was already halfway to the stairs. She'd guessed where Vic had gone. Webb, still cursing, came after her.

"Damn it, O'Reilly! You heard the Captain!"

"Not leaving the building, sir," she called over her shoulder. "I'm going after Vic."

Webb was older and in much worse shape than Erin. He finally caught up with her, huffing and puffing, just outside the interrogation rooms. Erin was working her way down them, glancing in the window in each door. She'd just found the one she wanted, room three, and reached for the handle.

"Don't," wheezed Webb.

She paused. "Vic's in there," she said. "With Ian Thompson."

"Great," Webb muttered. "Just great. Don't open that door. That's an order."

"Why not?"

"If you have to ask, you're a worse detective than I've ever thought you were."

Erin knew he was right. She was currently the subject of an Internal Affairs review. Ian was the only witness to the shooting. She couldn't talk to him until the review was concluded. It would compromise his testimony.

"Vic shouldn't be in there either," she protested.

"I know," Webb said grimly. "But he is. And better you than him. Now get yourself back upstairs."

"You're going to let him conduct an unsupervised interview? The way he is right now?"

Webb paused. Erin saw the indecision on his face. This time she was right. Vic was angry and unstable. But Webb also needed to keep an eye on Erin. With a growl of frustration, he threw open the door to the observation room next door.

"Get in there," he said. "And keep your mouth shut."

Erin obeyed, knowing she'd used up all the rope she was allowed for today. She and Webb had a good view of the interrogation room through the one-way window. Ian was sitting with his normal unnatural, alert stillness on one side of the table. Vic was standing on the other side, pacing like a restless bear.

"...don't get how much trouble you're in, do you?" Vic was saying.

Ian made no answer. He just watched Vic and waited.

"This is the second time you've murdered someone in front of a cop," Vic said. "You skated the first time. You think you can just go around New York killing people?"

"No," Ian said. "I followed the rules of engagement."

"You're not a damn soldier anymore!" Vic shouted, leaning over the table at him. "You're a criminal! You're just another dirtbag loser I've gotta scrape off the bottom of my shoe! You got one chance to save yourself, just one. What were you doing in that apartment?"

"Working." Ian's voice was completely calm. He didn't flinch when Vic got close to him, hardly reacted to him at all.

"What exactly does your job entail?"

"I drive Mr. Carlyle and protect him."

"By shooting women?"

"I'm licensed to carry. Ms. Finneran shot Mr. Carlyle and was going to shoot Ms. O'Reilly. I didn't initiate contact. I engaged only after shots were fired."

"Why was Carlyle there?"

"None of my business."

"What's he doing with O'Reilly?"

"None of my business."

"Your boss was fucking a New York detective. You say it's none of your business, but it's sure as hell my business, and that makes it your problem! You saying you're good with what's going on?"

Ian shrugged ever so slightly. "No complaints."

"Well I'm not okay with it!" Vic shouted right in his face.

"Sorry to hear that," Ian said coolly. "With time and therapy, you'll get over it."

Webb gave a startled snort on Erin's right. She glanced at him and saw that, in spite of everything, he was choking back a laugh. Vic, in the interrogation room, looked like he was strangling on his own anger.

"Will that be all?" Ian asked.

"You're going back to lockup, asshole," Vic snarled.

"Am I being charged with anything?"

"We can hold you overnight without charging you."

"Thanks," Ian said. "I could use some shut-eye. I guess I'll go back to my cell now."

Vic clenched and unclenched his fists. The man in front of him was hardly half his weight. He wanted to beat the crap out of him, intimidate him, get some sort of confession. But he couldn't hit him without committing a crime himself, Ian was impossible to intimidate, and the former Marine wasn't about to confess to anything. As far as Ian was concerned, he'd done nothing wrong. Muttering darkly, Vic put an arm on Ian's shoulder and propelled him out of the interrogation room.

"That's over," Webb said. "Now let's get back upstairs. We need to be there when the Bloodhound's finished with Holliday."

Chapter 17

"I need to make a phone call, sir," Erin said.

"No," Webb said.

"It's about Rolf. He's with my sister-in-law. She was expecting me to pick him up, hell, two hours ago. She's going to be worried sick."

"I'll call her and let her know you've been detained," Webb said. "Police business."

"Because that'll make her worry so much less, hearing that from someone other than me?"

"Sarcasm, O'Reilly? Now? I pity your dad when you were a teenager."

"Sir?"

"O'Reilly, I swear to God..."

"Never mind." Erin shut up. The moment she did, the fear came rushing back in. She remembered Carlyle's face, the horrible grayness of his skin, the bright red splash of blood. She kept thinking of him, and then Brunanski, dying of the same type of wound. She should be worried about her career, but right now, she'd trade her pension for his recovery. She wondered if God was in the mood to bargain. But she'd lose Rolf if she lost her job. There really was no good way out of this.

The minutes crawled by. The door to Holliday's office stayed shut. Erin worked on her paperwork, tried to wonder what scheme Keane was cooking up in there, and gave up on it. She was too worn down to care much. She wanted Rolf at her side, his warm, furry, reassuring presence. She wanted to sleep, to just pull a thick blanket over her head and blot out the world. Most of all, she wanted Carlyle. She wanted him the way she remembered him, clever, attentive, courteous. Not bleeding out, dying of shock and blood loss on her living room floor.

"Your sister-in-law, would that be the number we've got as your emergency contact?" Webb asked. "Sean and Michelle O'Reilly?"

"Yeah," she said dully.

Webb picked up his phone and dialed. After a moment, he said, "Mrs. O'Reilly? This is Harry Webb. Erin's commanding officer. I know she was supposed to pick up her K-9 this evening, but I'm afraid something urgent came up at the Eight. I've got her here. No, no, she's fine. Oh, no, ma'am, I'm sorry. She's engaged in police business right now and can't be disturbed. She just didn't want you to worry. Could you possibly hold onto Rolf a little longer? I'm not sure, it might be a while yet. Is there a time after which you don't want her to call? Okay, I'll tell her. You have a good evening, ma'am."

He hung up again and the waiting resumed.

Vic stalked into the office. He wouldn't look at Erin. Having him there felt like a great big weight dragging down that whole side of the room. He moped around for a while, not doing much of anything.

"Neshenko," Webb said. "Why don't you go home? We'll sort things out in the morning."

Vic grunted, stood up, and left.

Holliday's door swung open. Webb and Erin both looked up. Holliday was standing in the doorway.

"Come in, O'Reilly," he said. "Not you, Lieutenant."

Webb paused, confused. "Sir?"

"I'll let you know if we need you. For now, we just need O'Reilly."

Erin didn't know whether that was good news or bad news. She tried to put on her game face. Her whole body ached, as if she'd taken a beating. She was incredibly, unbelievably tired. She shuffled into the office on rubbery legs.

Holliday closed the door behind her. Keane was standing exactly where he'd been before, back against the wall, watching her.

"Are you all right, Detective?" Holliday asked. "Do you need something to drink? Coffee? Water?"

"No, sir," Erin said, even though her throat was dry.

"Sit down," Holliday offered.

"I'd prefer to stand, sir." In spite of her weariness, or maybe because of it, Erin didn't want to go down. She might not be able to get up again.

"Very well," Holliday said. "Lieutenant Keane and I have been discussing your situation. I believe we have a potential solution. Lieutenant, if you would?"

Keane had that mocking half-smile on his face again. "Here's the opportunity, Detective. Evan O'Malley's operation has been difficult for our Organized Crime Task Force to crack open. They've nibbled around the edges, but have never been able to really get inside. You have a direct line to O'Malley's number-two man."

"That's not exactly—" Erin began. She meant to explain that the O'Malley hierarchy was a little more fluid than that.

"Please, Detective, let me finish," Keane said. "Here's the way out. Mr. Carlyle will fully become an asset of the New York

Police Department. He will make a deal with the District Attorney in which he will agree to testify against his colleagues. You and he will collect information tying Evan O'Malley to his organization's criminal enterprises and build a RICO case to dismantle the O'Malleys altogether. You'll make a clean sweep and wipe them out completely."

"There's no way he'll agree to that," Erin said flatly.

"You have some influence over him, I would imagine," Keane said, still smiling his smile. Erin was starting to really dislike that expression. "Use it. Persuade him."

"And if he doesn't agree?" Erin asked.

Keane shrugged. "We don't have a case against him. He'll be released. Captain Holliday will accept your resignation from the NYPD. We all go our separate ways. We'll get Carlyle and the O'Malleys some other way, in due time. It's up to you, Detective. You have a choice, not only to save yourself, but to do something meaningful for this city."

"If he agrees?" Erin asked. "I see what's in it for me. What does he get? He'll want to know."

"I'll speak to the DA's office," Keane said. "Assuming Carlyle acts in good faith, I'm confident we can make a deal which will grant him immunity from prosecution for the numerous crimes he has doubtless committed." He paused. "Assuming, of course, he survives. If he dies, then our problem disappears."

Erin stared at him. "Meaning what, sir?"

Keane shrugged again. "We can't make a deal with a dead man, but if Carlyle doesn't survive, you're no longer concerned with the O'Malleys. Assuming your connection with them is entirely personal and based on your association with Carlyle, that is. In that case, you go on with your career as if nothing happened. All the preliminary evidence suggests it was a clean shooting this evening. You defended yourself against a home invasion by a known mob assassin."

Erin licked her lips and tried to moisten her throat. "It may take a little time to talk to Carlyle if... if he comes through surgery okay."

"Of course," Keane said. "I'd say forty-eight hours should be sufficient, assuming he regains consciousness and retains his faculties."

Erin searched Keane's eyes for any sort of empathy or human emotion and saw none. She'd always found Keane frightening and unpleasant. She hadn't truly begun to hate him until that moment.

"How's this going to work?" she asked. "Assuming everyone goes along with it."

"You'll be assigned a case agent," Holliday explained. "Not one from the Eight. It won't be someone you know personally. It'll be a guy with experience working with undercover officers and informants. You'll continue your normal duties, but you'll work concurrently with him. I have the right officer in mind. I've worked with him before. He's very good, and completely reliable. You will speak only to him, to Lieutenant Keane, or to me about this. Not one word to anyone else in the Department, nor to your family. I don't need to tell you the stakes involved, or what might happen if someone breaches security. You won't even discuss this with Keane or me unless it's an emergency. Do you understand?"

"Yes, sir," Erin said. In any other circumstances, this was the sort of assignment that would have thrilled her. Working in secret to take down a crime boss; it was the stuff of police legends.

"This has never been tried before," Keane said. "We've had undercover officers in the Mob, but never an openly-serving officer posing as a dirty cop. Your case agent will help you with the... gray areas you'll be encountering. You'll need some training and instruction."

"In the meantime," Holliday said, his face softening somewhat, "you have somewhere you need to be. You'll want to get back to Bellevue Hospital as soon as possible. Your assignment starts now."

"Yes, sir."

A little dizzy at the way the world had shifted around her, Erin left Holliday's office. Webb stood up from his desk and took a step toward her.

"Detective O'Reilly is free to go," Keane said from the doorway. "This matter is now concluded."

Webb stopped short. He clearly wanted to ask her something, but he closed his mouth. Erin walked past her boss and out of Major Crimes.

*   *   *

Erin hurried into the Bellevue Hospital emergency room, having detoured only long enough to pick up her car. She almost ran to the reception desk.

"Is Doctor O'Reilly out of surgery?" she asked.

"Not yet," the nurse said.

"Oh." Erin felt herself deflate again. She found a seat and got ready to wait some more. She had plenty to occupy her thoughts. Vic might never forgive her. Maybe he shouldn't. She wasn't sure she could forgive herself. Not if Carlyle died. She thought of every gunshot wound she'd seen in her twelve years on the Job, which ones had lived, which ones hadn't. She checked the clock. It was after ten.

If he survived, how could she convince Carlyle to betray the O'Malleys? He was an Irishman. He was no traitor. They didn't deserve his loyalty, but Erin had learned that being loyal was more about the person giving the loyalty than the value of the organization itself. It was important to Carlyle not to see himself as a traitor. But he'd agreed to turn Siobhan in. Maybe she could build on that. If he lived.

How dare Lieutenant Keane talk about him that way? As if his death would solve all Erin's problems. It would fix her life the same way a developer fixed a house by tearing it down to the foundation. She hadn't realized Keane was such a bastard. No wonder the other cops were afraid of him. She ought to tell Carlyle about that. He'd go on living just to spite that ambitious son of a bitch. If she ever got the chance to talk to him again.

And so it went, around and around her head. She picked up magazines and stared blankly at the pages for a while before putting them down again. She tried to sleep, but it didn't matter how tired she was. The sun had gone down, but the pale fluorescent bulbs in the ceiling kept shining. She checked the clock again. Ten thirty. More magazines. More thinking. Eleven o'clock. Twelve. Twelve thirty. Ambulances arrived. Bleeding people came through the ER. Old men with chest pains. Young kids with greenstick fractures. One o'clock. A long surgery meant he was still alive, at least. Burns. Lacerations. Midnight.

The door swung open and Doctor Sean O'Reilly came into the lobby. He looked exhausted. Dark bags were under his eyes. He looked around the room and saw Erin.

She jumped up and somehow found the energy to make it across the floor to her brother. "How...?" she began but couldn't finish the question.

"It was touch and go," Sean said. "We patched up the liver. He's lost a lot of blood. We pumped six units into him. He had a lot of internal damage. I got the slug out of him."

"But he's alive?"

Sean put a hand on her shoulder. "He's still critical, but stable. If he makes it through the next few hours, I think he'll pull through. I've done everything I can."

Erin wrapped her arms around her big brother and hugged him tightly. "Thank you," she said into his chest.

"Whoa, Erin, it's okay," he said, patting her awkwardly on the back. "Geez, you're supposed to be the tough one in the family." He drew back to arm's length and looked down at her. "This guy's really important to you, isn't he?"

"Yeah."

"Who is he? What's his name?"

Erin hesitated.

"Sis, I have to put something on his charts. What is this, some big secret?"

"Sean, it's complicated," she said. "Look, you're his doctor, right?"

"If you mean, am I the guy who just spent the last few hours saving his life, then yes, I am."

"This is confidential," she said quietly, glancing around the room. Fortunately, there was a lull. The only people besides the nurse at the reception desk were a mom and her little boy in the opposite corner. The boy was crying and his mother appeared completely absorbed in comforting him.

"Okay," Sean said.

"I mean, you can't tell Dad about this," she said. "Or Mom, or anyone else in the family. Not yet."

"Ah," he said. "Secret boyfriend?"

"Something like that."

"Isn't he a little... old for you, Erin?"

She gave him a look. "It's a fourteen-year gap, Sean. That's not the end of the world. He's in good shape."

"Too much information, kiddo," he said, making a face. "I do not need to know my kid sister's love life."

"It's just... there's some things about him. Dad might not understand. I need a chance to explain it to him. Without anyone jumping in and tipping him off."

"Okay, I promise," Sean said. Then he smiled suddenly. "Hey, you didn't tell Mom and Dad when you caught me making out in the back seat with Wendy Berkowitz back in high school. I told you I owed you for that one."

"It's never too late to cash in a favor, is it?" Erin said with a wan smile. "Thanks, Sean."

"So, his name?" Sean prompted again.

"Oh, right. It's Morton Carlyle. But can you keep him under a John Doe?"

"That seems a little excessive," Sean said. "I mean, Dad can be kind of a hard case, I know, but do you really think...?"

"Someone tried to kill him once this evening," Erin said. "I don't want anyone getting another crack at him."

"Oh," Sean said. "Of course. Sure."

"When can I see him?" she asked.

"Not tonight. I told you, he's in critical condition. He's certainly not taking any visitors. I'll check on him again in the morning. Go home, kiddo. Try to get some sleep."

"I can't go home."

"I know the waiting is hard, Erin. But you'll be more comfortable there than here."

"No, I mean, I can't go home."

"Why not?"

"It's an active crime scene. That's where he was shot."

Sean stared at her. "Jesus Christ. You didn't shoot him, did you?"

"Sean! What the hell do you think? Of course I didn't shoot him!"

"Just checking. Sorry. Hey, why don't you crash at my place? I'm pulling a double shift tonight, I won't be home. We've got an air mattress in the upstairs closet. We've been keeping your mutt for you, we might as well put you up, too."

"Okay," Erin said. "That'd be nice. But he's not a mutt." She didn't want to be alone, and she very much wanted to see Rolf. "Call there if anything changes, will you? I don't have my phone."

"Will do," he said. He kissed her on the forehead. "It's going to be okay, kiddo."

That was all it took to bring the tears to her eyes. "Dad always used to say that," she said. "Whenever one of us got hurt."

"And he never lied about it," Sean said with a smile. "Hang in there."

*   *   *

Anna and Patrick had been in bed for hours by the time Erin rang the O'Reilly front doorbell in Midtown. Michelle answered the door in fuzzy slippers and a bathrobe, looking tired but agitated. Rolf stood behind her, staring intently at the door. He'd been successfully de-ribboned. When he saw his partner, he didn't come running at her. He was no effusive Labrador. But his tail lashed so hard it sounded like someone smacking a baseball bat into the wall.

"Erin?" Michelle said. "Oh my God, what happened? You look awful!"

Erin wordlessly stepped into the front hall and her sister-in-law's arms.

"Are you okay?" Michelle asked. "My God, is that blood? I got the call from your boss. He sounded a little funny. Something happened, I know it did. It's written all over your face. Come in, I'll get you something warm. Tea or coffee?"

"Coffee," Erin said. "Cream, no sugar. Better make it decaf." She dropped to one knee and put her arms around Rolf's neck. He kept wagging his tail, a little more uncertainly. Erin didn't usually cling to him this way, and Rolf didn't like being forcibly restrained. But he was a good dog and he let her do it.

"Are you staying long?" Michelle asked from the kitchen. "Or did you just come for Rolf?"

"Overnight, if that's okay," Erin said.

"Sure," Michelle said. "Though it's halfway to morning already. But I don't understand."

Erin thought what she could tell her. "Someone broke into my apartment," she explained. "There was a fight. My... boyfriend got shot."

"Oh, Erin!" Michelle gasped. She was out of the kitchen before Erin could react, hugging her again. "I'm so sorry! Is it serious?"

"Yeah," Erin said. "But Sean operated on him. He thinks he may get through okay. But I can't sleep at my place. There's cops and police tape and everything."

"Of course," Michelle said. "This house is your house. Anything I can do. I mean it, anything."

"Right now, coffee's all I need. And somewhere to lie down. And this guy." She scratched Rolf behind the ears. He liked that much better than being clung to. He leaned against Erin's leg.

"Sure thing," Michelle said. She shifted into problem-solving mode. "I expect you'll want to get to the hospital again first thing in the morning. What do you want for breakfast?"

"Food," Erin said. Eating was just about the last thing on her list of priorities.

"You want to talk about it?" Michelle asked.

"Not right now. Maybe later."

"Just one thing," her sister-in-law said, unable to leave the subject completely alone. "You said there was a fight. Was he... protecting you?"

"He saved my life," Erin said.

Chapter 18

Erin didn't sleep much, or well. Rolf helped, a little. She came out of a semiconscious daze to find him resting his chin on her shoulder, his big, furry muzzle less than an inch from her face. When he felt her move, he lifted his head and stared soulfully at her.

She decided there was no point trying to sleep more. Michelle had laid out some spare clothes for her, a little too big but serviceable. At least they weren't covered with bloodstains. She checked the time; a little before five. That was good enough. She dressed and went into the kitchen as quietly as possible, not wanting to disturb the household. The cupboard contained a choice of oatmeal, cornflakes, or some sort of sugary kids' cereal that looked way too colorful to eat before noon. Erin put on the coffee and got a bowl of cornflakes. She wasn't really hungry, but knew if she didn't eat something she'd regret it.

While she was methodically working her way to the bottom of the cereal bowl, Erin heard movement. She looked up to see Michelle in the doorway.

"What else can I do?" Michelle asked softly.

Erin stood up. "If you wouldn't mind keeping Rolf a little longer? I'd like to have him with me, but I don't think they'll want him in the ICU. And I can't take him home."

"Of course," Michelle said. "You're going to the hospital now?"

"Yeah. I don't know for how long."

"It's okay, Erin," Michelle said. "I've got this. You take care of your man. Lord knows men wouldn't get far without us."

"Thanks, Shelley. For everything."

Erin's sister-in-law gave her a hug and a quick kiss on the cheek. "Hey, we're family, right? But you have to promise to let me meet this mystery man, once he's on the mend."

"I'll try," Erin promised. That was the best she could say. "I'll be back, kiddo," she added to Rolf, who looked skeptical.

* * *

Even in the city that never slept, emergency rooms tended to be fairly quiet before six in the morning. Erin approached the reception desk across an eerily deserted room. The nurse was different than the last time she'd been there.

"Erin O'Reilly, NYPD," she said, showing her shield. "I need to see Morton Carlyle. He's here under a John Doe."

"I'll need to call Doctor... O'Reilly," the nurse said, hesitating as she recognized the similarity in names. "Just a moment."

Erin waited while her brother was paged. Only a couple of minutes later, Sean emerged. He looked about the same as before; still tired, but still on his feet.

"What's his status?" Erin asked.

"He made it through the night," Sean said. "His vitals are pretty good, considering. We've upgraded him to Serious condition."

"Can I see him?"

Sean frowned. "It'd be better for him to rest."

"Not for long. At least let me look in on him."

"Okay. Come on back, kiddo."

Sean led her to a room with only one bed in it. There was Carlyle, IV tubes snaking out of his arm, machines beeping away. He had a hospital blanket pulled up to his chest, so she couldn't see the marks of the surgery. He looked very pale. His eyes were closed.

"God," Erin murmured softly. She didn't dare go into the room. They looked at him through the window that led to the hallway.

Sean put an arm around his sister's shoulder. "He's a lot better than he was," he said. "As long as we don't get a secondary infection, his chances are pretty good. He's in great condition for a man his... you know. Age."

"He's not that old, Sean," she said, elbowing him in the ribs. "Is he asleep?"

"I hope so. That'd be the best thing for him."

As if hearing their conversation, Carlyle opened his eyes and turned his head. His eyes were clear and aware. Erin saw the recognition in them and felt tears starting in her own eyes.

Slowly, Carlyle raised his hand and beckoned.

"I'm not going to be able to talk you out of this," Sean muttered.

"You'd need three big guys and a tranquilizer," Erin replied. "I won't... hurt him, will I?"

"Don't touch anything but his hand," Sean said. "Be gentle."

Erin opened the door and walked carefully across the floor, as if her footfalls might disturb the wounded man. A chair sat against the wall. She picked it up and set it down next to the bed, taking a seat beside him. She gently took his hand. It was still cool to the touch, but not as cold as she remembered from the previous night.

"How are you feeling?" she asked. A tear started rolling down her cheek. She ignored it.

His lips moved in a slight hint of a smile. "I feel like I've been to an Irish wedding, darling."

Erin's laugh came out almost like a sob. She cleared her throat. "They say you're going to be okay."

"Is that what they're saying? And there I was, getting my excuses ready for Saint Patrick."

"Saint Peter's the one at the Pearly Gates," Erin said.

"Ah, but the Irish go in through the kitchen door, around the back."

"You sound like Corky," she said, smiling through her tears.

"Siobhan," Carlyle murmured. "She's gone, isn't she."

"Yeah," Erin said. "She was going to shoot me, too. Ian and I..."

Carlyle nodded and closed his eyes. "I failed her."

"You did the best you could for her. She made her own choices. You told her so yourself. You said what she did was in her hands and on her conscience. Don't you start telling lies now."

"Did I say that?" Carlyle asked, opening his eyes again. "I don't deny I'm a bit foggy on the details. But I believe you. It's the sort of thing I'd say, and it's just like you to turn my words around on me. Who's that lad at the door?"

"That's my brother," Erin said. "He's the surgeon who patched you up."

"Grand. It's a pleasure to meet you, Doctor O'Reilly," Carlyle said, raising his voice slightly. "If I'd known another O'Reilly was to be tending me, I'd not have worried so."

"We do what we can," Sean said. "Glad to meet you, too, Mr. Carlyle."

At that moment, the intercom chimed. *"Doctor O'Reilly to Operating Room Two."*

"Back to work," Sean said. He hesitated. "Erin, don't go undoing all my hard work here. Go easy on this guy, and keep it short. Let the nurse know when you're done."

"Copy that, big brother," she said. "Go save lives."

Sean made a face she remembered from childhood and left. Erin watched him go. Then she carefully disengaged herself from Carlyle's hand, stood up, and went to the door. After a quick glance up and down the hall, she closed the door and returned to her seat.

"What's the matter, darling?" Carlyle asked. "Really, I'm grand. Just a few days on my back and I'll be back in the bloom of health."

"It's not that," she said. "It's... God, I don't want to hit you with this. Not now."

"What's happened?" he asked more sharply. He tried to pull himself upright, immediately regretted it, and went back down with a groan.

"They cut open your abdomen," Erin reminded him. "I wouldn't try to do any sit-ups."

"Aye, lass, I've just been reminded of that fact," he said through clenched teeth. "But what's happened with you?"

"They know," Erin said. "My bosses. The NYPD."

"Ah," Carlyle said. "They're certain?"

"Yeah. I told Captain Holliday. Lieutenant Keane, the Internal Affairs guy, knows too. So do Webb and Vic Neshenko."

"I've not made trouble for you, I hope," he said.

Erin shrugged. "They gave me a choice."

"Stop seeing me, or leave the police?" Carlyle guessed.

"Not exactly. They told me I could get you on our side, or resign."

"Meaning what, precisely?"

"You know what it means."

"What do they want me to deliver?"

"Everything. Evan O'Malley, his organization. They want to take the whole thing apart. Evan, Mickey Connor, Kyle Finnegan, Veronica Blackburn, all of them."

"No."

Erin was ready for this reaction, had expected it. "They don't deserve your loyalty. Some of these guys have tried to kill you before, and plenty of them would do it again. You can walk away from this, clean. They're offering you full immunity. From everything you've ever done for these bastards."

"In exchange for my life? You know what Evan's people will do."

"That's why we need to get all of them," she said. "Make a clean sweep and there'll be no one left to take revenge. You know who all these guys are. It'll take some time, but we can take them down from the inside."

"I'll not do it, Erin. I'm sorry. I can't."

"Is this about your code?" she demanded. She felt anger building inside her, made out of leftover fear and outrage. "What about me? What about my code? Do you know what I've risked for you?"

"Erin," Carlyle said, squeezing her hand with what strength he could. It wasn't much. "I can't hand Corky over. I'll die first. If my being alive is what's putting you in this fix, I'll wait till you're gone and pull these tubes right out of myself. I'll take my chances answering to the Almighty."

Erin had been afraid this would be his sticking point. But she had an answer ready. "What if we bring Corky in?" she asked. "Get him on our side? You're the reason he's here in the first place. You got him in with the O'Malleys."

"Corky's not like me, darling. He loves the Life. It's a part of him."

"You know it'll kill him," she said. "One of these days he won't be fast enough, or lucky enough, and he'll be dead. The only way to win is to walk away from the table after the right hand. You'll be saving him, too."

"Is this how you talk to your informants, darling? Is that what I'll be? Another tool for your department?"

"They'll see you that way. Just like Evan sees me as your tool now. We'll play both sides and we'll come out on top in the end. You and me. Corky, too. I can get Keane and Holliday to agree to that." Erin was about ninety percent sure of it. Then she smiled. "Now we're just discussing price."

Carlyle actually laughed, a shaky but genuine sound. Then he winced. "And there I was thinking this wasn't that sort of relationship. You can't be bought, darling."

"Neither can you. Not with money. Corky's your only real friend in the O'Malleys. Ian's your friend, too, and so am I. These others, they're not."

Carlyle nodded. "I'm well aware I've enemies in the O'Malleys."

"Think about it," she said. "We go away on a secret getaway to the Bahamas. The only people who know we've gone are the O'Malleys. When we come back, someone's waiting for me, with a gun, in my locked apartment. She knew where we'd been, Carlyle. Someone told her. They've already betrayed us, betrayed you. You didn't start this, but you can help me finish it."

He nodded again. "Aye, that stands to reason. We'd do well to consider that in the future." He looked closely at her. "So those were your options, darling? You turn me around, or you turn in your shield?"

"That's about the shape of it. They'd take my shield, my gun... and Rolf."

"There's always a third option. In every choice. What was it?"

Erin shrugged. "The third choice wasn't a choice. Keane said things might take care of themselves."

"If I died, you mean."

"Yeah."

Carlyle's face was thoughtful. Erin felt a surge of sudden panic. She clamped her hand hard around his fingers.

"No, damn it! You don't get to do that! You tried to die for me last night, Carlyle. I don't want you to die for me. I want you to live for me! I don't care how corny it sounds. You're mine, and I'm not letting you go!"

Carlyle's face tightened, then relaxed, and he looked calm, almost serene. "Then I suppose we've no choice," he said. "The decision's already made."

"What do you mean?"

He gripped her hand more tightly. "I mean I'm with you, darling. All the way, live or die."

Erin held his hand there in that hospital. All kinds of problems were waiting for them, enemies on both sides of the law. But somehow, looking at the weak, wounded man lying in front of her, Erin believed they could find a way through this mess. She took a deep breath.

"Okay," she said. "Let's do this."

Here's a sneak peek from Book 11: High Stakes

Coming March 2021

Erin started driving back to her brother's house in Midtown, but she was only about halfway when her phone buzzed with an unidentified number. That usually meant either Carlyle or a scam, and she knew Carlyle didn't have access to a phone. She almost let it ring, but a cop wasn't supposed to do that.

"O'Reilly," she said.

"You have a meeting with our guy. Can you get to Hell's Kitchen Park in half an hour?"

"Who is this?" Erin demanded. The voice was familiar but she couldn't immediately place it over the phone.

"Is this a secure line?" The voice turned slightly mocking.

That did the trick for her. *Keane, you son of a bitch,* she thought. "I think you'd know that better than I would, Lieutenant," she said.

Lieutenant Keane laughed softly. "Indeed I would. You're looking for a man wearing eyeglasses. He'll be sitting on a bench, by himself, doing the Times crossword."

"This guy got a name?"

"He'll tell you everything you need to know. Welcome to undercover work, Detective." Keane hung up.

"Bastard," Erin muttered. She glanced over her shoulder, reassuring herself with Rolf's quiet, intense presence. "You'd never rat me out to Internal Affairs, would you, partner?"

Rolf opened his mouth and let his tongue hang out over his teeth.

"Yeah, you're smiling now," she said. "This bullshit stops being funny when it starts being you."

She was partway to Hell's Kitchen already, since it lay right next to Midtown. It was traditionally the home of lower-class Irish in Manhattan, but Erin didn't know it well. The neighborhood had been heavily gentrified in the '90s, with housing prices rising to compete with its posh neighbors. Erin found the park easily enough with the aid of her onboard computer. She parked the Charger in a police spot and unloaded Rolf. They walked into the park together, Erin scanning the area for anyone fitting Keane's description, Rolf sniffing the air.

Growing up on a diet of Hollywood movies, she was expecting a shady-looking guy in a trench coat and fedora, or maybe a tough-looking Special Forces type with tattoos and scars. What she saw was a mild-looking man who looked to be in his mid-forties. He didn't look like a spy; he didn't even look like a cop. He was losing a battle with his waistline, which filled out a button-down shirt and blue blazer. He was clean-shaven and going bald. If he was wearing a gun, she didn't see one. But he was wearing eyeglasses and holding a ball-point pen in one hand, a copy of the Times in the other, and sitting on a park bench.

Erin walked slowly up to him, looking around for any backup or surveillance. She saw nothing out of the ordinary, but then, she'd have walked right by this guy on the street and assumed he was a civilian. He looked like he ought to be teaching high school civics, not waiting on a clandestine meeting with a detective.

He looked up from his paper, as if sensing her approach. Erin was a good judge of eyes and body language. His eyes were soft and thoughtful, his posture nonthreatening. He folded the paper and set it down on the seat beside him. He stood up and his eyes traveled quickly around the park. He was checking the same thing she had.

"Detective O'Reilly, I presume?" he said.

"Yeah," she said. "I was told I had a meeting with you."

He smiled. "Thanks for making the time." He held out his hand. "Phil Stachowski. I'm a lieutenant at Precinct 10, but don't bother with the protocol. I work with undercovers and informants, so I tend to be a little more informal than some. You can just call me Phil."

"Good to meet you," Erin said, taking the offered hand. He had a good grip, firm and steady. "Erin O'Reilly. This is Rolf."

"I've heard a lot about you," Phil said. "Can I call you Erin, or would you prefer O'Reilly?"

"Whichever," Erin said, managing to swallow the automatic "sir" she nearly put on the end out of habit. She was used to having a little latitude with her own lieutenant, but she knew Webb. Lieutenant Stachowski was a mystery to her, and the NYPD drilled its chain of command into its officers pretty hard.

"Erin, then," he said. "Have a seat. It sounds like we've got some things to talk about."

"Can I see some ID?" she asked. "Nothing personal, but this whole thing is kind of iffy, and I don't want to go off the rails any more than I have to."

He was still smiling. "Certainly, Erin. I see you already understand one of the primary principles of undercover work."

"What's that?"

"Everything's a test, all the time," he said. He flipped open his wallet and showed her what did, indeed, appear to be an NYPD Lieutenant's shield next to a driver's license that matched the name he'd given. "They're going to test you at every turn, sometimes deliberately, sometimes by accident. And unfortunately, you can pass ninety-nine out of a hundred and that last one can trip you up. Have you done undercover work before?"

"Not really," she said, seating herself on the other end of the bench. Rolf settled on his haunches next to her, eyeballing Phil. The Shepherd hadn't made up his mind about this whole thing either.

"I've read the O'Malley files," Phil said. "Captain Holliday sent them over to me last night. As I understand it, you've formed a personal connection with Morton Carlyle?"

Erin felt her jaw clench, but forced herself to relax. She'd have to get used to her personal life being discussed in tactical terms. That was part of the deal. "That's right," she said.

He nodded, and she realized that had been her first test. She wondered whether she'd passed.

"This Carlyle seems like a solid source in the O'Malleys," he went on. "He's an associate in good standing, and it appears he's one of the men in line to succeed Evan O'Malley. How did you get to know him?"

"I investigated him as a murder suspect last year," she said.

Phil laughed. It was a pleasant laugh, very natural. "Not a very promising start to a relationship," he said.

Erin smiled. "I saved his life and his place of business. He figured he owed me one. We started a business relationship, trading information and small favors."

Phil listened as Erin laid out the framework of how she and Carlyle had gradually come to trust one another. She described all the cases he'd helped with, the dangers they'd faced, the fights they'd been through side by side. When she was done, he leaned back and whistled softly.

"Holliday told me this was a little unusual," he said. "Normally, when we send someone to infiltrate an organized-crime racket, the whole point is that the target doesn't know our guy is a cop. But in this case, you're already known as a decorated detective. That brings both good and bad news with it."

"What's the bad news?" she asked, taking her cue.

"They know you carry a shield. They don't trust you."

"And the good news?"

"The operation can't be blown by them finding out you're a cop," he said with a grin. "You don't have to disguise *what* you are, only *who* you are. It's a difficult dance."

"How do you mean?" Erin asked.

Phil leaned forward. His eyes were dark brown, and as he looked at her, Erin saw that under the surface softness he had an intensity to him. "A lot of undercover officers think the worst danger is that they'll get found out, that someone will shoot them. And you do need to be careful about that, but you're obviously an experienced and sensible officer, so I won't insult you by harping on that point. The worst danger, Erin, is that you can get lost in the role. You can forget who you are and what you're trying to do.

"The hell of this job is, you need to make friends with people, get them to like you, even love you, while planning to destroy them. If you do your job right, when we put the cuffs on them and put them in interrogation rooms, they won't give up your name because they'll still think you're on their side, and they'll want to protect you. You need to earn their loyalty and betray them. Not everybody can do that. Can you?"

"I think so, yeah," Erin said, with one inner reservation. She wasn't going to betray Carlyle.

Phil's posture relaxed slightly. "Good. Hey, Erin, it's going to be okay. This is serious, we both know that, but I've run plenty of undercover ops before. I'm going to be your liaison. This is Captain Holliday's operation, but you're not to go to him with anything unless it's an absolute emergency and you can't reach me."

"Yeah, Keane told me that," Erin said.

"And you don't go to Keane with anything," Phil said. "Not unless Holliday and I are both out of the picture."

"Why not? Because he's Internal Affairs?"

"Because I know Andrew Keane," Phil said. "He's a politician. That means he's ambitious and inherently untrustworthy. The more people who know about what you're doing, the more chance there is of this going sideways. Ideally, I want this to be you, me, and your contact. Here's a phone."

He slid an old-school cheap flip-phone along the bench toward her.

"I'm programmed in, my contact listed as Leo."

"Nickname?" Erin guessed.

"Sign of the Zodiac," he said with a smile. "You can call me anytime, for any reason. I'll answer or return your call within half an hour. I'll be drawing up a plan of action for us. As long as this Carlyle is cooperative, it should be pretty straightforward. He'll be doing all the heavy lifting."

"There's a wrinkle," Erin said. "He's in the hospital right now."

"So I hear," Phil said, nodding. "That's no worry. We're in no particular rush. You never want to rush an undercover op. When people rush is when they make mistakes. For now, I just needed to meet you, talk to you face-to-face. Make sure you're up for this."

"To see if I'm up for this?" she repeated, raising an eyebrow.

"Exactly," he agreed. "I think we'll work well together, Erin. I'll be in touch. Keep this phone near you, charged, and turned on. If you don't answer, I'll assume you're okay. I won't leave messages, nothing that would compromise you. You're on the sharp end on this; there's no emergency on my end that's ever going to justify using you as an emergency contact for me."

He stood up. "Glad we've had this talk. Do you have any questions for me?"

Erin had so many she didn't even know what to say. But one of them floated to the top of her consciousness. "Does this sort of thing work? I mean, are we going to be able to pull this off?"

"It usually goes okay," he said. "Just keep your mind on what you're doing, and remember who you are."

"I never forget," she said.

*   *   *

Erin finally got back to the O'Reilly house, just in time for dinner. She smelled the food as soon as she opened the door; Mary had obviously spent the afternoon making her famous pot roast. Erin glanced down at her partner and smiled. Rolf was too proud to beg, but the Shepherd's body was betraying him. A thin strand of drool was working its way from his jowl toward the floor.

The whole O'Reilly clan had assembled. Erin's three brothers were all there; Sean Junior, Michael, and Tommy. Michael's wife Sarah was talking with Michelle, while Anna and Patrick played some sort of game on the living room floor involving a wooden train set and a small herd of pastel-colored toy horses. Tommy had his guitar out and was meditatively picking out a melody. Erin's dad, in the middle of it all, was placidly reading the Times. Michael, next to him, had appropriated the Business section of the paper.

Mary came bustling out of the kitchen. "We're just about ready," she said. "Oh, Erin! There you are, dear!"

"Rolfie!" Anna shouted and charged toward Rolf with her arms wide. The K-9 had faced down armed felons. He'd been shot, Tased, and beat up. He didn't flinch from the little girl's squealing onslaught, just giving Erin a look of long-suffering patience as Anna wrapped her arms around his neck.

"Gang's all here," Erin said.

"It isn't often we all get together," Michelle said. "Sorry. I should've warned you."

"It's okay," Erin said. "Hey, family are the people you can't get rid of, right?"

"Depends," Tommy said. "I bet you know a guy, right, sis? Know any good hitmen?"

Erin's dad slowly lowered his paper and gave her a meaningful look.

She pretended not to see it. "If I do, Tommy, you'll be the first one I'm sending them after."

"Tommy O'Reilly sleeps with the fishes," he said, doing his best Godfather impression, which wasn't a very good one.

Dinner was a raucous affair. Erin let the rest of her family carry the conversation. She had a lot on her mind. Phil Stachowski seemed like a nice guy, but a nice guy wasn't what Erin needed. She needed someone competent, someone who would have her back. At least he wasn't pissed off at her like the entire rest of the NYPD. And then there were the Irish to consider. What had Ian told Evan O'Malley? What would Evan do? Would he hold her responsible for what had happened to Carlyle? Or had it been his plan all along, to kill both of them?

"You need to keep up your strength, dear," Mary said.

"Huh?" Erin hadn't been paying any attention.

"You're just pushing your food around your plate. Did I mess something up? I thought pot roast was one of your favorites."

"It is. Sorry. It's just..." Erin didn't know how to finish the sentence.

"Don't badger her, Mary," her dad said quietly. "She's had a rough time."

"Of course," Mary said. "I just thought some comfort food might help."

Erin saw tears in her mother's eyes and felt suddenly bad for her. Mary was trying to help the best way she knew, and she didn't know the whole story. Erin forced herself to concentrate on the taste of the food, the way it warmed her on the way down. After a while, she really did feel a little better.

After dinner, Anna and Patrick played with Rolf for a while, before being hauled up to bed with sleepy protests. The adults talked and drank coffee. Erin heard some of Sean Junior's funny medical stories, some of Michael's boring business stories, and some of Tommy's bizarre musician stories. She and her dad contributed a few police anecdotes. It was a pleasant enough evening that she was able to almost forget all the crazy chaos that was waiting for her.

About ten thirty, the other O'Reilly siblings said their goodbyes, exchanged hugs, and left for their own homes; Michael and Sarah's swanky downtown apartment and Tommy's Greenwich Village loft which he shared with three to five other musical types, depending on the state of their finances.

"Did you smell reefer on Tommy?" Her father whispered in Erin's ear.

"Yeah. You want to talk to him about it?"

He shook his head. "No point. That kid's gonna do what he does. I just wish he'd get a real job."

"You mean, a job where you get shot at?" Erin asked.

"I mean a job that pays actual money. Guitar won't get you anywhere. For every Elvis, there's a thousand guys playing on street corners for spare change."

"Dad, do you ever stop worrying about your kids? We're grown up now."

"Never. You'll find that out if you ever have kids of your own." He sighed. "Little pieces of your heart running around, making bad choices, getting in trouble. And you wonder why I've got such a big gun cabinet."

"You can't shoot everything that comes after us, Dad."

"A man can dream." He put an arm around her shoulders. "I even worry about you, kiddo, and you're the toughest of the bunch. I guess a girl with nothing but brothers is either gonna grow up safe and sheltered, or tough as nails."

"If I have to choose, I'll take the nails," she said, putting an arm around her dad in return.

"That's my girl."

Erin's phone buzzed. She fished it out and saw Webb's name. "Great," she muttered, then hit the answer icon on the screen. "O'Reilly."

"Got that paperwork done yet?" Webb asked.

"I'll have it for you tomorrow, sir," Erin said. "Like I promised."

"Not if you're not done yet," he said.

"What do you mean?"

"You're back on the clock. We just caught a body. Not too far from your place, actually." He gave the address.

Erin's heart skipped a beat. "That's right next to..."

"The Barley Corner, yeah," Webb said. "The alley behind it. Go on and get to the scene. You'll probably be there before we do. Neshenko's got a bit of a drive."

"I'm not at home," she said. "I'm at my brother's, in Midtown. But I can be there in twenty."

"Copy," Webb said. "See you there."

"Work?" Sean asked as she hung up.

"Yeah. Back to work."

"You okay, kiddo?"

"Always."

* * *

It might be a coincidence, Erin told herself. The Corner had a lot of Mob activity around it. Maybe it had nothing to do with Carlyle's shooting. Maybe it wasn't even a homicide. People dropped dead on New York streets all the time. Heart attacks, seizures, car accidents.

She kept repeating comforting theories to herself all the way down. At least it couldn't be Carlyle himself. He was in a hospital bed under police guard. Besides, he didn't hang out behind the pub. The back door of the Corner was steel core and protected by a state-of-the-art security system. It had nothing to do with him.

She parked the Charger with the other police vehicles already on scene. She didn't see an ambulance. Either the EMTs had come and gone, or the state of the body had made it obvious their services wouldn't be required. She unloaded Rolf and headed for the alley, flashing her shield to a couple of Patrol officers who were standing guard at the entrance.

The smell hit her right away. It was like copper, almost, but with an organic undertone. The scent of blood was impossible to mistake for anything else. She also caught a faint whiff of gunpowder. That meant the scene was fresh, certainly less than an hour old. Up ahead, she saw a couple more uniforms standing with their flashlights trained on the body. It was behind a dumpster. She could see the feet sticking out, clad in brown leather shoes and jeans.

"What've we got here?" she called to the officers.

"Single victim," the sergeant in charge of the scene said. "White male. Two GSW, one in the hand, one right through the forehead. Exit wound damn near took off the back of his head."

"Ouch," Erin said. She walked around the dumpster, keeping Rolf on a short lead. The Shepherd sniffed at the man's foot and went into his alert posture, indicating the presence of a dead body. Erin's gaze traveled up the corpse, starting at the feet. Nice shoes, but not overly fancy. Fairly new jeans. A white button-down shirt, dirty and stained with blood and alley debris. The man was heavyset, with a big gut. His right hand was covered with blood, a pool of it soaking into his pants. He'd taken a bullet there for sure. He had a gold necklace with some sort of Celtic charm on it. Erin let her eyes finally rest on the dead man's face.

The bottom dropped out of her stomach. "Shit," she whispered.

"Yeah," one of the other cops agreed. "Not a nice way to go. At least it was quick."

Erin hoped the flashlights wouldn't show how pale her face probably was. She thought she might throw up. It wasn't the fact of the body, or the way the man had died.

"We haven't ID'd him yet," the sergeant said. "If it was a robbery, he won't have his wallet. But maybe facial recognition..."

She shook her head. They wouldn't need facial recognition. She knew the dead man. And his death meant all kinds of trouble.

Caleb Carnahan, Carlyle's chief of security, lay dead behind the building it had been his job to protect. His eyes, wide open and staring, showed a last instant of shocked disbelief. A splatter of blood was sprayed across the brickwork behind his head like a ghastly halo.

Ready for more?

Join Steven Henry's author email list
for the latest on new releases, upcoming books and
series, behind-the-scenes details, events, and more.

Be the first to know about new releases in the Erin
O'Reilly Mysteries by signing up at
tinyurl.com/StevenHenryEmail

About the Author

Steven Henry learned how to read almost before he learned how to walk. Ever since he began reading stories, he wanted to put his own on the page. He lives a very quiet and ordinary life in Minnesota with his wife and dog.

Also by Steven Henry

Ember of Dreams
The Clarion Chronicles, Book One

When magic awakens a long-forgotten folk, a noble lady, a young apprentice, and a solitary blacksmith band together to prevent war and seek understanding between humans and elves.

Lady Kristyn Tremayne – An otherwise unremarkable young lady's open heart and inquisitive mind reveal a hidden world of magic.

Robert Blackford – A humble harp maker's apprentice dreams of being a hero.

Master Gabriel Zane – A master blacksmith's pursuit of perfection leads him to craft an enchanted sword, drawing him out of his isolation and far from his cozy home.

Lord Luthor Carnarvon – A lonely nobleman with a dark past has won the heart of Kristyn's mother, but at what cost?

Readers love *Ember of Dreams*

"The more I got to know the characters, the more I liked them. The female lead in particular is a treat to accompany on her journey from ordinary to extraordinary."

"The author's deep understanding of his protagonists' motivations and keen eye for psychological detail make Robert and his companions a likable and memorable cast."

Learn more at tinyurl.com/emberofdreams.

More great titles from Clickworks Press

www.clickworkspress.com

The Altered Wake
Megan Morgan

Amid growing unrest, a family secret and an ancient laboratory unleash long-hidden superhuman abilities. Now newly-promoted Sentinel Cameron Kardell must chase down a rogue superhuman who holds the key to the powers' origin: the greatest threat Cotarion has seen in centuries – and Cam's best friend.

"Incredible. Starts out gripping and keeps getting better."

Learn more at clickworkspress.com/sentinel1.

Hubris Towers: The Complete First Season
Ben Y. Faroe & Bill Hoard

Comedy of manners meets comedy of errors in a new series for fans of Fawlty Towers and P. G. Wodehouse.

"So funny and endearing"

"Had me laughing so hard that I had to put it down to catch my breath"

"Astoundingly, outrageously funny!"

Learn more at clickworkspress.com/hts01.

Death's Dream Kingdom
Gabriel Blanchard

A young woman of Victorian London has been transformed into a vampire. Can she survive the world of the immortal dead—or perhaps, escape it?

"The wit and humor are as Victorian as the setting... a winsomely vulnerable and tremendously crafted work of art."

"A dramatic, engaging novel which explores themes of death, love, damnation, and redemption."

Learn more at clickworkspress.com/ddk.

Share the love!

Join our microlending team at
kiva.org/team/clickworkspress.

Keep in touch!

Join the Clickworks Press email list
and get freebies, production updates, special deals,
behind-the-scenes sneak peeks, and more.

Sign up today at clickworkspress.com/join.

CPSIA information can be obtained
at www.ICGtesting.com
Printed in the USA
LVHW082028161121
703475LV00021B/850/J